Scott was suddenly aware that Alicia was on her own for the whole night.

The kids had always been a buffer against his growing desire for Alicia, but now there was only Alicia. An empty house. And hours and hours of the night still ahead.

He shook his head. *Very bad idea.*

He should make an excuse and leave her to enjoy the solitude alone. But then their eyes locked.

The moment was instantly shattered by the beep of the smoke alarm and smoke billowing out of the oven. They stood there in the middle of the kitchen, laughing like a couple of idiots over the demise of a loaf of garlic bread.

And she just looked so beautiful, with her eyes sparkling and her cheeks glowing, he couldn't resist.

He kissed her.

Dear Reader,

I've always been fascinated by family dynamics: the interactions between husbands and wives, fathers and daughters, brothers and sisters.

A family is a collection of individuals—and individual personalities. And sometimes those personalities will clash. There may be conflicts and controversies, miscommunications or misunderstandings, politics and power struggles.

But at the heart of family is…heart.

That's why I was so thrilled to be invited to participate in this series.

One Man's Family is the story of Scott Logan, a man who feels as if he's never quite fit into his own family, and Alicia Juarez, a woman who has put her dreams on hold to raise her brother's family. It is a story about their journey together, about how they open up their hearts and discover what family really means.

Thanks for opening the book and joining Scott and Alicia on their journey.

Enjoy!

Brenda Harlen

ONE MAN'S FAMILY

BRENDA HARLEN

SPECIAL EDITION

Published by Silhouette Books

America's Publisher of Contemporary Romance

Special thanks and acknowledgment
are given to Brenda Harlen for her contribution to the
LOGAN'S LEGACY REVISITED miniseries.

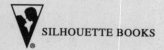 SILHOUETTE BOOKS

ISBN-13: 978-0-373-24827-8
ISBN-10: 0-373-24827-X

ONE MAN'S FAMILY

Printed in U.S.A.

BRENDA HARLEN

gave up a career as a family law attorney to be a stay-at-home mom and pursue her dream of writing romance novels. She soon learned that there isn't much staying at home for a mom of two busy children but has no regrets about the choices she made. Sometimes she even finds time to write.

The award-winning author lives in Southern Ontario with her husband and two sons, whom she credits as the inspiration for all her happily-ever-afters.

Readers can write to Brenda c/o Silhouette Books, 233 Broadway, Suite 1001, New York, NY 10279, or via e-mail at brendaharlen@yahoo.com.

To my Dad—
because every little girl needs a hero,
and because you'll always be mine.
I love you.

Prologue

"In the matter of the State of Oregon versus Joseph Elonzo Juarez…"

Alicia held her breath, straining to hear the words over the pounding of her heart. The jury had been deliberating less than twenty minutes, and she couldn't help but feel reassured by the quick decision. Clearly the jurors had seen beyond the flimsy and circumstantial evidence and knew that her brother hadn't committed any crime.

"…we find the defendant…"

Her grip tightened on the railing in front of her, her short fingernails biting into the lacquered wood, her attention fixed on the jury foreperson.

This was it. Finally. The end of a seemingly endless four-day trial, and the beginning of a return to normalcy for her family.

"…guilty."

She couldn't hold back her shocked gasp as her gaze flew across the courtroom to where her brother was standing beside his attorney at the defendant's table.

Joe's shoulders were slumped with the weight of the world upon them, but he looked more resigned than surprised by the announcement. She, on the other hand, had to fight the urge to yell at him, to scream at the judge and rail at the jury for this blatant miscarriage of justice. Except that nothing she could say or do would make a difference now.

She felt a gentle tug on her sleeve and looked down into the wide, trusting eyes of her eight-year-old niece.

"Is Daddy coming home now?" Lia asked.

Before Alicia could say anything, Joe Jr. responded with all the disdain a twelve-year-old boy could muster for his little sister. "He's not ever coming home, dummy. 'Guilty' means he stays in jail."

Alicia shot her nephew a warning glare over the top of Lia's head before kneeling beside her niece. The little girl's eyes were filled with tears and confusion. Alicia knew just how she felt, but she couldn't give in to the emotions that battled inside her. She was the only one these children had to look out for them right now.

"But he didn't do it." Lia's bottom lip quivered as she spoke.

"I know, honey," she said, trusting with all of her heart that it was true. "The jury just made a mistake."

"Tell them," Lia pleaded. "Tell them they were wrong, Aunt Alicia."

The child's fervent pleading broke her heart, but it was too late to tell the jurors anything. Having been thanked and dismissed by the judge, they were already filing out of the courtroom.

And it wasn't Alicia's job to convince them of Joe's innocence. That was something *he* should have done. But her brother had chosen not to take the stand, had refused—for reasons he didn't even try to explain and that she couldn't begin to imagine—to defend himself.

"Tell them," Lia said again.

Alicia only wished it were that easy.

She would do anything for these children, give them anything. But what they needed most of all was their father, and his fate had been sealed by the jury's announcement.

Or had it?

Chapter One

Scott Logan had things on his mind and a crick in his neck, both courtesy of having spent the better part of three days hunkered down in the front seat of an aging Ford Escort on an insurance fraud investigation. Despite the mental preoccupation and physical discomfort, he felt good about the successful completion of another assignment and satisfied that he'd done his job well.

His former colleagues couldn't understand why he'd walked away from the police force for this kind of work, and Scott didn't know how to explain that the job that had once meant everything to him had meant nothing after Freddie was killed.

His family, who had never comprehended his wanting to be a cop in the first place, understood his new job even less. Not that they criticized his choices so much as they were clearly baffled by them. In a family comprised of mostly white-collar professionals, Scott had always been the odd man out.

You can do anything you want to do was Lawrence Logan's favorite mantra, and one which he repeated at every opportunity to each of his four sons. It was the kind of positive and nurturing approach he'd advocated in the self-help books that had brought him so much fame and fortune. His encouragement and support were genuine, his pride in his sons' accomplishments sincere.

He'd flown to New York to help LJ settle into his new apartment when his eldest son had accepted a position with a prestigious public relations firm, had been sitting in the front row when Ryan graduated with his architectural degree, and cried tears of joy when Jake was accepted to medical school. But when Scott announced his intention to go to the police academy, the renowned psychologist had just shaken his head—as he'd done frequently over the thirty years of his youngest son's life.

Scott hadn't been deterred by his father's lack of support because there had been no other options for him. He'd wanted only to be a cop—to uphold the laws, put the bad guys in jail and help make the world a safer place. Of course, when his partner was killed—gunned down in pursuit of an armed suspect who was later acquitted on a technicality—Scott's faith in the system was shaken.

He banished these disquieting memories to the back of his mind as he pushed open the door to Darlene's Diner. The bell tinkled, announcing his arrival, and Darlene herself glanced up from the counter she'd been wiping down to greet him with a smile.

"Morning, stranger."

"How are you, Darlene?"

"Hanging in," she told him. "How about you?"

"Desperately needing my daily dose of caffeine."

She was already reaching for a large foam cup. "You haven't been in the last few days."

"Assignment," he said simply.

She glanced up at him again as she filled the cup. "You been sleeping in your car again? You look like hell."

"I haven't been getting much sleep," he admitted. "Regardless of where I spend my nights."

"You need a good woman, sugar. A reason to go home at night." She set the coffeepot back on the element and winked at him. "And lots of steamy hot sex that wears you out so good you can't help but sleep."

"Is that an invitation?"

Darlene threw back her head and laughed. "Sugar, you wouldn't know what to do with me if I said yes."

"How will we ever know, if you don't give me a chance?"

She snapped a lid onto the cup and slid it across the counter to him as the bell tinkled over the door again and another customer entered.

"Because despite your broad shoulders and tough-cop scowl," she told him, "you've got a heart softer than the yolks of sunny-side up eggs, and I eat guys like you for breakfast."

He frowned at that. "You must be confusing me with someone else."

"Actually, I was thinkin' it was an appropriate—if somewhat bizarre—analogy," another female voice piped in from behind him.

Scott turned to see Aster Cooney, proprietor of the

local salon and spa, slide onto a stool at the counter. Her hair, pink and purple today, was sticking out in tufts around her face, her eyelids were covered in glittery lime-green shadow and her lips were painted orange. In a denim miniskirt that hugged her round hips and a lime green T-shirt, she should have looked ridiculous. But somehow she managed to appear almost stylish, if a little flamboyant.

"Good morning, Aster," he said, inwardly cursing himself for lingering to flirt with Darlene.

Not that he didn't like Aster. On the contrary, she was one of his favorite people in the world—open and honest and incredibly gutsy. And he usually enjoyed her company, but he felt at a distinct disadvantage now, knowing that she and Darlene would gang up on him over some issue or another.

"You're gettin' an early start today," Aster said. Then she turned to Darlene. "Decaf vanilla latte and a toasted cinnamon raisin bagel with cream cheese, please."

"I've been out of the office for the last three," he told her, as Darlene turned away to take care of the new order. "Lots of paperwork to catch up on."

"You look tense," she said, not unsympathetically. "I could squeeze you in for a massage around three, if you want."

"I'm fine," he said.

"I was just telling Scott how he needs a woman's hands on him," Darlene told Aster, then grinned. "Only I wasn't talking about a back massage."

Aster nodded her agreement. "That might be just what he needs—but only if it's the right woman."

Today, the topic of their interest was his personal

life—or rather his lack of one. He admittedly hadn't dated much since breaking up with his long-time girlfriend a couple years earlier, but that was his own choice. And he had no intention of sticking around for their diagnosis of his dating problems because he was perfectly content with his life.

"Thanks for the insights, ladies," he said, tossing a couple of bills onto the counter. "But I'm already behind schedule and really need to run."

"You should do that," Aster surprised him by agreeing. "Because the way she kept glancin' at her watch, I doubt she'll wait much longer."

"She—who?" Darlene asked the question before he could.

"The gorgeous dark-haired woman who's standin' outside the door of his office buildin'."

Scott frowned. "She isn't waiting for me."

Aster shrugged. "Even if she isn't, she just might be the one you've been waitin' for."

"Aster," he said warningly.

"Go on. You can tell me later that I was wrong—" she grinned "—or not."

Scott left the diner certain that Aster was wrong.

He knew he didn't have any appointments this morning because he'd asked his secretary to clear his schedule for the entire week, not sure how long he'd be tied up with the insurance investigation. His only pressing concern now, and the reason for his early arrival at the office, was dealing with the paperwork and e-mails and telephone messages that would have piled up during his absence. But maybe one of the other investigators—

The thought fizzled abruptly when he rounded the

corner of the building and saw her standing there. And in the back of his mind came the assurance that Aster wasn't wrong about one thing: the woman was gorgeous.

His police training kicked in to make a more detailed assessment: Hispanic, five feet four inches tall, a hundred and twenty pounds, approximately twenty-five to thirty years of age. Long, dark hair tied into a braid that fell to the middle of her back, darker eyes, wide full lips, and dressed in hospital scrubs with white running shoes on her feet. It was an impartial and professional appraisal, but what came next was a purely involuntary and completely male evaluation: sensual, seductive, sexy.

She was petite, and he usually liked his women taller—long and leggy. But she had curves that would make any man's mouth water and lips that promised a taste of paradise. Though the punch of arousal that hit low in his belly was unexpected, it wasn't unwelcome. It was always good to know that he was alive and well, that his body wasn't dead even if his heart had long ago been buried beneath the unforgivable weight of grief and guilt.

"Scott Logan?" she asked, when he stepped closer.

"Yes."

His hesitant response was immediately rewarded with a warm smile, and he felt a quick rush of heat through his veins.

She really wasn't his type. But there was something about her that called to him on a primal level—or maybe it was just that Darlene and Aster's teasing remarks in the diner had reminded him that it had been a very long time since he'd been with a woman.

"I was afraid you wouldn't get here before I had to leave for work," the woman said.

Her voice was as soft and seductive as her smile, and he almost didn't hear the words he was so caught up in the enjoyment of the sounds rolling off of her tongue. Then he realized she was waiting for him to say something, and he forced his brain to wrestle control away from his suddenly overactive hormones to respond to her statement.

"Do we have an appointment?" he asked, starting to question his earlier conviction that they did not. Maybe Caroline had booked it after he'd called yesterday afternoon to tell her that he'd be in the office this morning.

"No," she admitted. "But I was hoping you could squeeze me in, anyway."

He glanced at his watch, as if he were considering the request. But the truth was, he was intrigued enough by the woman to want to listen to whatever she had to say. Especially if she continued to speak in that smoothly melodic tone that made him think of steamy nights and steamier sex.

Whoa. He immediately reined in the shockingly unprofessional thought, surprised—and a little ashamed— at the purely visceral reaction he was having to this woman. It was Darlene's fault, he rationalized again. He wouldn't be having such inappropriate ideas if she hadn't started him thinking about how long it had been since he'd had a woman in his bed.

"Why don't you come in?" he offered, inserting his key into the lock.

She waited until he'd punched in the code to disarm the security system before she followed him through the door. He flipped on lights as he made his way toward his office at the end of the hall, conscious of her presence behind him, wondering what had brought her here so early in the morning.

Did she want him to check up on a spouse whom she suspected was unfaithful? He hadn't seen a ring on her finger, but he knew that wasn't conclusive evidence of anything. And while securing evidence of infidelity wasn't one of his favorite assignments, it was, regrettably, a regular one. Still, he had to wonder at the stupidity of a man who could have a woman like this one in his bed and still look elsewhere for pleasure. Of course, it wasn't his place to speculate or judge, only to do the job he was hired to do.

He settled in behind his desk and pushed the stack of unopened mail aside.

"I'd offer you coffee, but this—" he held up his foam cup "—is all I've got until my secretary gets in. Caroline's very proprietary about the coffeepot."

She lowered herself onto the edge of one of the visitor chairs facing his desk and folded her hands in her lap. "I'm fine, thanks."

Scott took a long sip from his cup, hoping the infusion of caffeine would jump-start his brain and help keep it one step ahead of his hormones. "Why did you want to see me?"

"I need you to get my brother out of prison."

The unexpected statement jolted him even more than her presence, followed quickly by a pang of disappointment.

"I'm sorry, Miss—"

"Juarez," she said. "Alicia Juarez."

He paused, wondering why the name sounded vaguely familiar even though he was certain he'd never met this woman before. He had no doubt that he would have remembered.

"Yes, well, Miss Juarez, you're obviously at the wrong place. If you're looking for a bail bondsman—"

"I'm not," she insisted. "I need *you*."

He wanted to smile. Unfortunately, as much as he enjoyed hearing those words come from her lush lips, he was sure she didn't mean them the way he wanted her to mean them.

She huffed out an exasperated breath when he didn't respond to her announcement. "I thought Mr. Hall was going to talk to you about this."

Mr. Hall—now *that* name was definitely familiar. "Jordan sent you here?"

"He recommended you to me—" and it was clear from her tone now that she was wondering why "—and promised he would give you the background on Joe's case."

"I apologize for not making the connection sooner," he said, as the scattered pieces finally clicked into place in his mind. "I only talked to Jordan last night and while he did mention you would be contacting me, I didn't expect it would be first thing this morning before I've even had my first cup of coffee."

"I did intend to make an appointment," she told him. "But when I called yesterday, your secretary said you'd been out of the office and I should call back today. I thought, instead, I'd try to catch you in person on my way to work this morning."

"And you did."

She nodded. "Did Mr. Hall tell you about my brother?"

"Joe Juarez," he said. "Convicted of stealing an engine

prototype and its design plans from the racing team he worked for and sentenced to five years in prison."

"He was set up."

"Whether he was or wasn't..." Scott said—and he had his doubts "...what do you think I can do?"

"Prove his innocence," she responded immediately.

"The police already investigated the case, your brother had a trial, and the jury convicted on the evidence presented."

"But he didn't do it," she insisted.

"I appreciate your loyalty—"

"It's more than loyalty," she interrupted. "It's the truth. I know my brother. He simply isn't capable of doing something like this. And even if he was, he wouldn't do anything that would even risk taking him away from his kids."

Scott couldn't deny that she was convinced of the fact. Unfortunately, his experience in law enforcement suggested an entirely different scenario: if Joe Juarez was in prison, that was most likely where he deserved to be.

"You don't believe me," she said softly.

"It's not my job to believe or disbelieve," he told her.

"How can you do your job if you don't believe in your client?"

"Actually, I don't do a lot of investigating anymore. Most of what I do is surveillance."

"Oh." She frowned. "But Mr. Hall said that you were the best person for the job."

Scott bit back a sigh as he realized that whatever Jordan had said to this woman, she'd believed it— probably as easily and completely as she believed in her brother's innocence. He silently cursed his cousin's wife's brother for dragging his name into this mess. And then he cursed himself, knowing that he wouldn't be able to say no to this woman with the big, dark eyes that so clearly projected the hope and faith she was placing in him.

Still, he tried, because he really didn't want to be responsible for dimming the light in those eyes. "I'm not sure I am the best person for the job."

Her chin lifted, just a fraction, and her mouth set. "Are you saying you won't help me?"

"I'm saying, I'm not sure that I can help you," he corrected gently. "What if the only evidence to be found proves that your brother should be in jail?"

"I don't believe that," she said stubbornly.

"It's a possibility you have to consider."

"Then *you* have to consider the possibility that he was wrongly convicted."

He had to respect her persistence. "Touché, Miss Juarez."

"Will you help me, Mr. Logan?"

Damn, he really wished he could say no. The business was successful enough that he could mostly pick and choose his assignments these days, and he usually chose to work with big, faceless corporations, where the only thing at stake was money. He certainly wouldn't have chosen a client who looked at him with such trust and vulnerability in her eyes and her brother's liberty at stake.

But she had chosen him, and he found that he couldn't turn her away.

"I'll try," he finally responded to her question.

And the smile she gave him was so full of warmth

and pleasure, it would have knocked him off his feet if he hadn't already been sitting down.

"Mr. Hall said you would need a retainer," she said, already pulling a checkbook out of her purse, as if she was determined to finalize their agreement before he changed his mind.

Scott nodded.

The firm's standard contract asked for a retainer of ten thousand dollars, but he knew that Jordan had handled Joe Juarez's case through Advocate Aid, which meant there was no way she had that kind of money at her disposal. He would have to severely slash his usual hourly rate and work fast to get this job done on a budget this woman could afford. "Is fifteen hundred agreeable?"

Her surprise was obvious and followed quickly by relief. She nodded. "That would be fine."

Scott pulled up the contract on his computer, changing the retainer fee and hourly rate on the form with a few quick keystrokes while she wrote out the check.

"You know I can't guarantee you the results you're looking for," he said, as he passed her the contract to review.

She nodded again. "I'm only asking you to do your job, Mr. Logan. The results will speak for themselves."

He would do his job, and he knew that he would sincerely regret it if the results of his investigation destroyed her hopes for her brother's freedom.

Alicia left the Children's Connection at the end of her shift with a much lighter step than she'd started the day with. Her spirits had taken a decidedly upward turn when Scott Logan agreed to look into her brother's conviction. Despite his initial reluctance, she instinctively trusted that he could find the necessary evidence to exonerate Joe.

For the first time in weeks, she felt as if there was hope, and Scott Logan was responsible for that.

Unfortunately, the P.I. was responsible for stirring other feelings inside her, too. Like the unmistakable warmth of sexual attraction that spread heat through her veins when he looked at her with deep brown eyes that reminded her of the sinful temptation of dark melted chocolate. Or maybe it was the obvious strength in his broad shoulders that appealed to her at this time in her life when she so desperately needed someone to lean on.

The thought brought a rueful smile to her lips as she pulled into the designated parking space outside her apartment building and shut off her engine.

She didn't like to lean on anyone and wasn't in the habit of doing so. But she could imagine herself leaning on Scott Logan—and enjoying it, despite a track record with men that was both pathetically short and sad.

She hadn't been involved with anyone since her disastrous relationship with Ross Harmon more than three years earlier. And, truth be told, she hadn't felt as if she was missing out on anything. Or maybe she'd been so devastated by Ross's betrayal, and so angry with herself, that she'd accepted the denial of her own wants and needs as punishment for her error in judgment.

But no matter how attractive Scott Logan was—and he was, undoubtedly, *very* attractive—there were too many other things going on in her life to even contemplate a relationship. And right now, she needed to pack up more of her clothes and personal effects to take to her brother's house.

She felt a pang of sadness as she stepped into her apartment and looked around. It wasn't spacious or fancy, but it had been her home for the past three years. She'd moved in when she'd started her job at the fertility clinic linked to the Children's Connection, taking over the lease from another nurse who was getting married because it was an easy—albeit intended temporary—solution to her housing dilemma.

She'd stayed because she'd genuinely liked the neighborhood and her neighbors. There were the Walkertons, a young couple with a four-month-old baby; the Racines—Harriet and Abe—who'd been married almost sixty years and, if Myrtle Grossman was to be believed, fighting all of that time; Marissa Alonzo, a single mother who juggled three jobs to support her three children; Ronald Tedeschi, an engineering student at PSU; and Ingrid Stavros, her seventy-year-old landlady who baked cookies for every tenant on his or her birthday.

Alicia ignored the tightness in her throat as she shoved the last of her clothes into her duffel bag. She'd been living at her brother's house since his arrest, taking care of his children, and though she loved Joey and Lia more than anything, she really missed the eclectic group of tenants who had somehow become her extended family. And she missed her home—her private haven that was comfortable and familiar and entirely her own.

As she zipped up the bag, she pushed her petty

regrets aside. She had no right to complain about giving up her home when her brother had lost everything.

Besides, if Scott Logan was as good as his reputation, she wouldn't be gone for long.

He can't find evidence that isn't there, Jordan had warned her. *But if there's anything the cops missed, he'll uncover it.*

Alicia was counting on that. More importantly, Lia and Joey were counting on it.

Thinking of her niece and nephew, she hefted the stuffed bag onto her shoulder and headed back outside to her car. She waved to Myrtle Grossman across the street as she tried to recall if she'd taken anything out of the freezer for dinner that night. Steak, she remembered now. She'd planned to make a stir-fry—one of her nephew's favorites and one of the few ways she knew to get him to eat vegetables.

She had her key in hand to unlock the trunk when she noticed something written in the dust on the back window. One of the neighborhood kids—probably Marissa's eldest son, she guessed, although she'd never actually caught him in the act—seemed to think it was funny to write WASH ME on her vehicle when it was obvious that Alicia had neglected to do so.

But this time the message said: BACK OFF.

She felt a chill skate over her skin despite the late afternoon sun beating down on her.

It wasn't just the words that were different, it was the style of lettering. Bigger and bolder.

Or was she wrong?

She'd been uneasy since Joe had gone to prison, jolting at noises in the night, jumping at shadows. She was overreacting, letting her imagination get away from her, envisioning dangers where there were none. No doubt this was another example of the same thing.

The message probably wasn't even intended for her, but for the driver of whatever vehicle might find itself behind her on the road. And the logic of this reasoning soothed her skittish nerves.

Until she noticed the slashed tires.

Chapter Two

Scott arrived at Alicia's apartment complex less than fifteen minutes after her call.

He recognized Detective Mel Rucynski from his years on the force and greeted his former colleague with a firm handshake.

"What are you doing here?" Rucynski asked.

"Alicia called me."

"Alicia, huh?" Rucynski lifted his thick black eyebrows. "Well, your taste in women has definitely improved in the past couple of years."

The cop's suggestive tone made Scott realize he'd slipped in referring to Alicia by her first name, as he'd slipped throughout the day whenever thoughts of her came to mind. And although those thoughts had been anything but professional, focusing on her as a woman rather than a client—a woman with dark sparkling eyes, wide full lips, and temptingly round curves that he wanted to feel pressed against him—he didn't want Rucynski to get the wrong idea about his relationship with Alicia.

"Actually, Miss Juarez is a client," he said, reminding himself as well as Rucynski of that fact.

"A client, huh?" the cop asked doubtfully. "Well, if she has enough money to call you out to investigate a juvenile prank, she should have enough money to move out of this neighborhood."

"What kind of prank?" Scott asked, ignoring the dig about his fees. A lot of his former colleagues assumed he'd made the jump to the private sector to fatten his wallet. And while he did take home a heftier paycheck now, it wasn't money that had motivated the switch.

"Slashed tires." Rucynski gestured to the parking lot behind him.

Scott looked over his former colleague's shoulder and saw an ancient red Jetta in one of the few occupied slots. "Slashed tires" was something of an understatement, he thought, noting that the vehicle was actually resting on its rims because the tires had been so completely decimated.

"Looks like an unusually violent prank," he noted.

Rucynski shrugged. "Some kids are carrying around a lot of anger."

He nodded. It was an act of vandalism, possibly—probably—random, and yet there was something about it that bothered him.

"What did you tell Al—Miss Juarez?"

"The truth—that this neighborhood isn't exactly

upscale, and the fact that she's lived here for three years without incident is only proof that she was due for some trouble."

"What about the words on the back windshield?"

"By her own admission, the neighborhood kids sometimes leave messages in the dust on her car."

Scott nodded, but he wasn't convinced.

Not that he blamed Rucynski for looking for an easy answer. He'd responded to too many of these same types of incidents when he'd been in uniform, and usually the simplest explanation was the right one. But he'd also learned to trust his instincts, and his instincts were warning him that this might not be as straightforward as Rucynski wanted it to be.

"Is that going to be the conclusion of your report?"

"We'll ask around, see if any of the neighbors saw anyone or anything suspicious. But at this point, yeah, I can't see that it will play out any other way.

"I know that won't satisfy your..." Rucynski paused deliberately "...uh, client, but the truth isn't always what we want it to be."

Which was exactly the same point Scott had tried to make when he'd talked to Alicia about investigating her brother's case earlier, and he anticipated that she'd still be as resistant to it as she'd been then.

She responded immediately to his knock, and he saw that she'd changed out of the scrubs she'd been wearing earlier that day and into a pair of softly faded jeans and a simple scoop-neck T-shirt. Her hair was still in a braid, but her feet were now bare and her toenails, he noted with surprise, were painted blue and decorated with tiny white and yellow daisies.

Obviously there were layers to the woman he hadn't suspected, layers that he was curious to explore.

"What did Rucynski tell you?" she asked without preamble.

"Probably the same thing he told you—that it looks like a juvenile prank."

She folded her arms across her chest and paced across the threadbare carpet. There was an old—possibly even antique—couch against one wall, decorated with colorful pillows in various geometric shapes. Beside it was a newer-looking wing chair and ottoman. The coffee table looked sturdy, if scarred, and held a neat stack of magazines. Facing the couch was an ultra-modern entertainment unit of glass and aluminum that housed a small TV and modest stereo system, along with stacks of CDs and DVDs.

It was…eclectic, he decided. And yet somehow warm and appealing—like Alicia herself.

He turned his attention back to the woman who was still pacing.

The protective instincts that had sent him racing across town in response to her phone call rose up again and urged him to go to her, to wrap her in his arms and promise to take care of her. But he managed to resist the impulse, recognizing that holding her wouldn't just be inappropriate but potentially disastrous for his peace of mind. After only one meeting with the woman, he'd already found himself daydreaming about her. God help him if he touched her and found she was as soft and warm as he imagined her to be.

No, there could be no personal contact. He needed to remember that she was a client, off-limits, and to keep his distance. But that was tougher than he wanted to admit when she had her arms wrapped around her middle to disguise the fact that she was trembling.

"I can understand why this has shaken you—"

She turned abruptly to face him. "I'm not afraid of whoever slashed my tires."

He frowned. Whoever had done that number on her car had been wielding a dangerous instrument. Hell, *he* was scared just thinking about the possibility that Alicia might have interrupted the culprit in the middle of his task and had the weapon used against her.

"I'm just furious that the cops think they can brush me off with statistics about the incidence of crime in this neighborhood." She resumed her pacing, taking less than a dozen steps to move from one end of the room to the other, then pivoting on her heel to change direction.

"Rucynski assumed it was a prank at first glance and decided there was no need to dig any further." She turned again, her eyes fairly sparking with fury as her gaze met his. "If those are the kind of cops who investigated my brother's case, no wonder he's in prison."

He stepped into her path, forcing her to either stop or run into him. "Did you call me to complain about the apparent ineptitude of the police, or was there another reason?"

She huffed out a frustrated breath. "I'm sorry," she said. "I just hate being spoken down to, and Rucynski did everything but pat my head."

"He isn't the most diplomatic cop I've ever known, but his instincts are usually good."

"Well, I don't believe for a minute that this was a random act of vandalism."

"What do you think it was?"

"A threat—to stop me from looking into the charges against Joe. Think about it," she said. "My car getting trashed the same day I hired you is just too coincidental."

"You really believe there's a connection?"

"It's the only explanation that makes any sense," she insisted.

"Did you tell anyone about our meeting this morning?" he asked.

She shook her head. "After I left your office, I went straight to work, and I've never talked to anyone there about my brother's situation."

"Was there anyone who knew about your plan to meet with me?"

"Just Jordan. And your secretary."

And it was unlikely that either Jordan or Caroline would have shared that information with someone who could be responsible for the damage done to Alicia's vehicle. Which, if this wasn't a random act, forced him to consider another possibility—that Alicia had been followed.

Before he could ask any more questions, she glanced down at her watch, then turned away from him. "I'm sorry to drag you out here then have to take off," she said. "But I'm already late and the kids will be wondering where I am."

"How are you going to take off without any tires on your car?"

"I'll call my mechanic to have it towed and take a cab to my brother's place."

"Call for the tow," he said. "I'll give you a ride home."

* * *

Alicia was surprised by his offer—and tempted to decline.

She was a woman who prided herself on not needing a man for anything, but the truth was, she couldn't help her brother on her own. She *did* need Scott's help. And he'd already come through for her twice today. The first time when she'd shown up at his office without an appointment, and the second when she'd tracked him down on his cell phone to tell him about the incident with her car.

So she set her pride aside again and responded, "That would be great. Thanks."

He waited while she called her mechanic and didn't say a word or express the slightest hint of impatience when what should have been a two-minute conversation turned into a much longer one while Ernie pried the details of the situation from her and expressed indignation for her car's plight.

"Sorry about that," she said when she'd finally hung up the phone.

"Not a problem," Scott said easily. "Are you ready to go now?"

She nodded and reached for her duffel bag at the same time he did. Their fingers brushed and she jolted at the contact, instinctively pulling her hand away as he said, "I've got it."

She felt as if she should protest, but didn't bother when she saw how easily he slung the bag over his shoulder. The same bag she'd wrestled with to get it down the stairs to her car earlier, and then back up when it became obvious that she wasn't going anywhere in her own vehicle.

She followed him out the door, her mind moving ahead to the various tasks waiting for her at her brother's house.

Child care wasn't just cooking dinners and packing lunches, she'd soon realized. It was getting the kids out of the house in time for the school bus in the morning, then chauffeuring Lia to her piano lessons and ballet classes and Joey to his track-and-field practices and soccer games after school. There was also homework to oversee, tests to study for and bedtimes to enforce, all the while trying to ensure that the children were adjusting— as if anyone could adjust—to their father's absence.

Scott unlocked the passenger door of a sparkling powder-blue sportscar and tossed her bag into the backseat before stepping back for her to slide in. She did so, almost sighing with pleasure as the butter-soft leather enfolded her in its embrace. He closed the door for her, then went around to take his seat behind the wheel.

As he turned the key in the ignition, the engine roared to life. His hand settled over the gearshift, his broad palm gently cupping the knob, his long fingers resting casually against the stick. He shifted gears and pulled away from the curb, the vehicle slipping smoothly into the stream of traffic.

Great hands, she thought, then tore her gaze away from the man and focused on the car.

"I would imagine it's difficult for a private investigator to blend in driving something like this," she said.

"I have another car for blending," he told her. "This baby is for pure pleasure."

"I can imagine," she said, running a hand over the sleek contour of the dash. "Wow."

"That's exactly what I said the first time I saw her," he admitted.

"Her?"

He shrugged. "The most beautiful things in the world are female."

"And that includes a classic 1966 Corvette Stingray?"

"You know cars," he said, sounding surprised.

Now it was her turn to shrug. "My brother has a knack for anything with an engine, and I picked up a few things here and there from hanging around the garage with him when we were kids."

She fell silent, thinking about her brother and happier times. And she wished, more than anything, that he could be here with her now. He would love this car. More, he would love to be on his way home to be with his son and daughter instead of depending on her to take care of the children who meant the world to him.

"I'm guessing you picked up more than a few things," Scott said. "And I have to wonder how a woman who can appreciate a spectacular machine like this could be satisfied driving a tin can on wheels."

"My little car has been getting me where I need to go for the past eight years," she told him.

"That doesn't answer my question."

"The answer is economics. My paycheck goes to rent, food, tuition, books and—every two weeks—a tank of gas."

"Tuition?"

She squirmed in her seat. She didn't usually talk about her schooling. In fact, no one other than her family and her supervisor at work even knew about the courses she was taking. "Med school," she admitted.

"Impressive."

"Have you requested the transcript from Joe's trial yet?" she asked, determined to move the focus of their conversation back to her brother's case.

"I left a message for the court reporter today, but she hasn't got back to me yet."

"Oh." Alicia wasn't really surprised, but she was disappointed.

"And I talked to Jordan," he continued. "He's going to get your brother to sign a release so he can give me copies of everything in his file. Then, when I know what evidence the court had, the names of the witnesses who testified and what they said, as well as everything your brother told his attorney, I'll be able to determine the best direction for my investigation."

She had been one of those witnesses, and she cringed at the memory of her appearance in court. She'd blamed Joe for not taking the stand, but she'd realized—after the fact—that she'd made as big a mistake in choosing to testify. And when Scott read the transcript, he would know how badly she'd screwed up.

She was relieved when he turned onto Greenleaf Drive, as anxious to abandon the topic of the trial as conversation about med school. "It's the fourth house on the right."

She saw his eyebrows rise as he pulled into the driveway and noticed the plastic menagerie that lived in the front flower bed: the trio of faded pink flamingos, the banjo-strumming frog and flute-playing pig, and the cow wearing denim overalls and a straw hat.

"Interesting decorations," he said.

"Thanks." He hadn't turned off the engine, and she guessed that it was his intention to make a quick getaway. While there was a part of her that urged her to let him go, acknowledging that she'd intruded on his time enough already, there was another part—indoctrinated by her mother—that insisted she offer him a meal in appreciation of his trouble. "You'll stay for dinner, won't you?"

Before he could respond, she was out of the car and halfway across the front yard toward the neighbor's house.

"I just need to get Joey and Lia," she called over her shoulder to him when she heard the engine finally shut off. "They're next door with Mrs. Harbison. Then I'll be right back to get dinner started."

Scott had no intention of staying.

Although he appreciated the invitation—and he was more than tempted by the prospect of an actual home-cooked meal—he needed to remember that Alicia was a client. And sharing dinner with a client, when that client was a beautiful woman who stirred desires too long dormant, was dangerous—even with two children as chaperones.

Two children who were obviously surprised and none too pleased by his presence.

"Lia and Joey," Alicia told him, indicating her niece and nephew in turn. Then, to the kids, "This is Mr. Logan."

"So?" the boy asked.

Alicia's gaze narrowed on him. "So say hello."

"Hi," he muttered with obvious reluctance after another moment's pause.

"Hi," Scott said back, still wondering how to extricate himself from this awkward situation as Alicia opened a side door and led the way into the kitchen.

The little girl followed her aunt but kept her eyes—as dark and beautiful as Alicia's despite being red-rimmed from crying—on him.

"You were late," she finally said accusingly.

"*I* was late," Alicia corrected her, laying her hand on the refrigerator door to keep it closed when she saw her nephew reaching for the handle.

"I'm going to start dinner now," she told Joey. "And I know you had a snack at Mrs. H.'s, so you can wait twenty minutes to eat a proper meal."

Then, without missing a beat, she returned to the conversation she was having with her niece. "And I would have been even later if Mr. Logan hadn't given me a ride home."

But Lia clearly wasn't placated by this explanation. "You promised to be here when I got home from school."

"I know I did, but I had a flat tire on my car. And you know that if you ever get home and no one's here, you're supposed to go to Mrs. H.'s—just like you did today."

"But you promised." The little girl's eyes filled with tears again.

And Scott, who had almost no experience with kids and even less with female tears, felt for the child who had obviously dealt with too many broken promises of late.

"I'm sorry," Alicia said, immediately followed by, "Joey, come back here," to the boy who had snuck out of the room when he thought she wasn't looking.

"Okay," Lia responded, more than willing to forgive now that her feelings had been acknowledged.

Scott just stood back and watched Alicia handle the kids, impressed by the effortless way she anticipated their actions and responded to their needs. It occurred to him that this might be the perfect time to make his excuses and effect an escape. But he was afraid she'd call him to task the same way she'd done with her nephew's attempted defection.

"Any homework tonight?" Alicia asked, stroking a hand over the girl's hair.

"Math, but Mrs. H. helped me with it."

"Good, then you can go upstairs to practice the piano."

"Okay." And the child skipped off and up the stairs, her earlier displeasure already forgotten.

"What about you?" Alicia asked, turning her attention to the older brother who stood with his arms crossed and a scowl on his face.

"What?" her nephew asked.

"Do you have homework?" she prompted patiently. The kid shrugged. "Some."

"Did you do any at Mrs. H.'s?"

"Nah. Me and Randy were playing Nintendo."

"Then you'd better get to your homework now."

"But *Class of the Titans* is on TV."

"You should have thought of that when you were playing Nintendo with Mrs. Harbison's grandson instead of doing your homework."

"Homework's stupid," he said.

"No it's not, but you will be if you don't do it."

Joey rolled his eyes as he picked up his backpack and headed into the living room.

"Not in front of the TV," Alicia told him.

"I can't believe how much my life sucks," the kid

muttered as he changed course and carried his backpack into the dining room.

"I can," Alicia responded evenly. "But it could be a lot worse—and will be if you don't start cooperating."

Scott was momentarily taken aback by her cavalier response, then realized she knew exactly what she was doing with each of the kids. Lia was obviously feeling uncertain and insecure and Alicia was giving her the comfort and reassurance she needed. Joey needed a firmer hand to prevent him from acting out the anger and frustration he was holding inside, and his aunt was making it clear that she was in charge and wasn't going to take any attitude from him.

Apparently the petite nurse had a lot more going for her than a pretty face and hot body—she understood these children, and was determined to help them adjust to the recent changes in their lives.

But who was helping her? he couldn't help but wonder.

And why did he suddenly feel the urge to plant himself firmly in her corner, to let her know she could count on him?

"Sorry about that," she said, turning back to him. "The kids are still having a difficult time adjusting to Joe's absence."

"I'd guess that's normal," he said.

She smiled wryly as she reached into the fridge, coming out with a package of steak and a bag of vegetables. "As if anything about the situation is normal."

"You're worried about them," he guessed.

"Of course." She found a glass cutting board and selected a long knife from the butcher block on the counter, then began slicing the meat into thin strips. "Probably

Joey more so than Lia, because he isn't as open about his feelings as she is. She's sad and she's hurting, but she expresses her emotions—sometimes quite passionately—and gets over it. Joey keeps everything bottled up inside and I'm not sure that anything I say or do can help because, bottom line, I'm not his father."

"Does he see his father?"

"He did last week." She set a deep frying pan on the stove, drizzled some olive oil into it and turned on the burner beneath it. "I didn't realize the intake process would take so long—more than four weeks—and that was the first chance we had to visit since he was transferred to Columbia River Detention Center."

"How did it go?"

"Not good. Lia cried through most of the hour, Joey barely said two words, and Joe and I just stared at one another feeling helpless."

The oil sizzled when she dumped the meat into the pan. "I wish I could believe it would get better, but I'm not sure that it will, and those kids have done nothing to deserve this."

She dumped the board and knife into the sink, then turned on the tap and scrubbed her hands with soap and water. "Then again, I don't believe Joe did anything to deserve his fate, either."

She dried her hands on a towel, then found another board and knife and started slicing a red pepper into thin strips.

He watched her move around the kitchen, impressed by the efficiency with which she worked, and glad that he was sitting here watching her make dinner instead of on his way back home.

He tried to remember the last time a woman had offered to cook for him and couldn't. He knew it had been more than two years because that was how long it had been since his ex-girlfriend moved out. And it had been a rare occasion for her to prepare a meal that didn't come ready-made for the microwave. She hadn't liked to cook and he'd understood that she didn't feel like hovering over a stove after spending ten or twelve hours at her job. And yet, here was Alicia, not only undertaking the task at the end of what he knew had been a long and difficult day, but making it look easy.

"I wasn't going to stay for dinner," he told her.

She smiled as she sliced briskly through a zucchini. "You have to eat, and I had to cook for myself and the kids, anyway."

"You look like you enjoy cooking."

"I do," she said, moving on to peel the carrots she'd set aside. "Even when I'm only cooking for myself, it relaxes me."

She took a couple of cans of soda from the fridge, offered him one. "I'm glad you decided to stay."

He noted that she started when their fingers brushed in the transfer, as she'd done when he'd reached for her bag back at her apartment. Was she just jittery? he wondered. Or was she also feeling the sparks generated by the energy between them?

"You didn't really give me a choice," he said, leaving the chemistry issue aside for now. "And maybe I should thank you for that, because I would have gone home to a frozen dinner with only my TV for company."

She stepped away from him, turning to stir the meat

and vegetables in the pan. "It's always more fun to share a meal with a friend than to dine alone."

He popped the top on his drink. "Are we going to be friends, Alicia?"

"I hope so."

Scott was starting to hope—against his better judgment—that friendship would only be the start.

Chapter Three

Alicia knew she had a tendency to talk too much when she was nervous, and she found herself rambling throughout the meal and even after. Scott Logan, on the other hand, seemed to be a man of few words. He answered the questions she asked and responded to statements directed to him, but he did so with a minimum of words and always managed to redirect the conversation back to her.

It was a disconcerting change for Alicia to sit across the table from a man who didn't regale her with stories designed to prove how interesting or important he was. Her most recent dating experiences had been with men who, though expressing an interest in her, were really more interested in themselves. She didn't know many who would have hung around to dine with two ill-behaved children and even fewer who would have stuck it out through after-dinner negotiations over TV shows and bedtimes. So she was more than a little surprised to return to the kitchen after running Lia's bath to discover that Scott Logan was not only still there but washing dishes.

Of course, this wasn't a date, so she really shouldn't compare the P.I. with the other men she'd dated. But she couldn't deny there was something about the image of a strong man with his hands immersed in sudsy water that made her heart skip a beat. Forget candlelight dinners and long-stemmed roses—a man who willingly tackled household chores was the one who scored points with her.

"When I invited you to stay for dinner, I didn't expect you to help with the washing up."

"I don't mind," Scott said, wiping the cloth over another plate.

"Well, as much as I appreciate the effort, my mother would be appalled if I let an invited guest do my dishes." She nudged his hip with her own to push him aside so that she could take over.

Of course, the subtle hip check didn't even seem to register, except maybe in the glint of humor she saw in his dark eyes when he turned to meet her gaze. "In case you didn't notice, I'm a lot bigger than you."

"I noticed," she admitted. "But my brother taught me not to be afraid of someone's size. 'The bigger they are, the harder they fall,' he always told me."

"That might be true," Scott said. "But it would be easier for you to find a towel and dry these dishes instead of battling with me over washing them."

She shrugged as she retrieved a clean towel from under the sink. "If you really want to help, I'm not going to refuse."

"But it goes against your grain, doesn't it? And not just because of your mother would disapprove."

"What do you mean?"

"You strike me as a woman who feels compelled to do everything for herself, maybe just to prove to yourself that you can, or maybe because there hasn't been anyone around to lend a hand."

His words struck painfully close to the truth. "Were you a psychologist before you became a private investigator?" she asked.

One side of his mouth quirked up in a half smile. "No."

"That's right, you were a cop," she said, remembering what Jordan had told her.

"Yeah, but my father's a psychologist."

"And you think that gives you license to perform an amateur analysis of my character?"

"No," he denied. "But I am curious."

"About psychology?"

"About you," he said. "About how a woman who already juggles a full-time job and med school ended up with legal guardianship of her brother's children."

"He asked," she said simply. "And there was no one else."

"Their mother isn't around?"

"Joe was granted full custody in the divorce," she said. "That should tell you something about Yvette."

"Grandparents?"

She shook her head. "Yvette cut all ties with her parents a long time ago. I don't even think the Solomons have ever seen their grandchildren."

"What about your parents?"

"They died almost four years ago."

"I'm sorry," he said sincerely.

"There was a fire in the restaurant they owned. They lived upstairs. I know it probably sounds weird, but I actually found comfort in the fact that they were together. They'd been married forty-two years and devoted to one another for all that time."

She slid open the cutlery drawer, dropping in forks and knives as she dried them.

"They were the reason I got interested in reproductive technology," she continued. "Because my mom suffered through so many miscarriages, both before and after Joe and I were born.

"She and my dad always said they wanted a dozen kids, but it took a lot of years before she finally had Joe. Then, when she had me less than a year and a half later, they thought their luck had turned around.

"But I was the end of the line, and although we never had reason to doubt how much they loved us, we knew they were both saddened by the loss of the other babies she couldn't carry to term."

"So now you help other women have the families they want," he said.

She nodded. "Not all of our patients get the results they want, but for those who do...well, it really is a miracle."

"And for those who don't?"

"It's just one more heartbreak," she admitted.

"It must be hard dealing with those emotional highs and lows."

His insight and understanding surprised her, and made it impossible for her to hold back. "A while ago, I was reprimanded by one of the doctors who caught me crying in the staff room. She said that tears were unprofessional and I had no business working at the clinic if I couldn't hold myself together."

"That was harsh."

"Dr. Logan thought so, too. He—" She narrowed her gaze on him. "Dr. Jake *Logan?*"

"My brother," he admitted.

"I should have guessed," she said. Jake was a little taller and Scott's shoulders were a little wider, but otherwise the physical resemblance was striking.

"You were telling me about crying in the staff room," he reminded her.

"And your brother came in and interrupted Dr. Morningstar's lecture to tell me that, in his opinion, compassion was more important than professionalism. Then he handed me a box of tissues and steered Dr. Morningstar outside so I could finish crying in peace."

She allowed herself a smile before admitting, "I cry a lot—tears of sadness and despair when a procedure fails, tears of happiness and gratitude when one of my patients experiences the joy of giving birth."

He rinsed the stir-fry pan, then pulled the plug. "Does Dr. Morningstar still give you a hard time about that?"

"She transferred to another clinic a couple of months ago—just after the Sanders adoption case hit the headlines."

"That was a nasty one, wasn't it?" He wiped around the inside of the sink as the water swirled down the drain.

"I'm not sure it's over yet." She put the pan away and folded the towel. "Now Robbie Logan—" She paused.

"My cousin," he told her.

"Okay. Robbie has resigned and apparently disappeared, and there are still rumors that the agency might close."

Despite her boss's reassurances that they would weather this latest scandal, Alicia was concerned. Not just for the patients who desperately needed the hope the clinic offered, but for herself personally. If the Children's Connection shut down, she'd lose not just the job she loved, but her means of supporting herself and her brother's children.

"I thought LJ's campaign had turned things around."

"LJ?"

"The PR guy who was brought in from New York to help spin things for the media—LJ Logan," he explained. "Another brother of mine."

"How many of you are there?" she wondered aloud.

"Four. LJ's the oldest, then there's Ryan—he's an architect—then Jake, and myself."

"Four," she echoed. "I'll bet you kept your mother hopping."

"She blamed us for every one of her gray hairs."

She smiled. "What is it like, being part of a big family?"

"It's crowded," he said. "And noisy. But it's fun, too."

"You're close to everyone?"

"Mostly," he said, and left it at that.

"Joe and I have always been close," she said, turning on the tap to fill the coffeepot with water, then dumping it into the reservoir. "And now—" she shook her head "—I just can't believe any of this is happening."

He didn't offer any platitudes, for which she was grateful. There was nothing anyone could say that would make her current situation any easier to accept. There was no way anyone could understand what it was like for her brother to be locked away in prison, knowing he shouldn't be there.

Still, she couldn't stop herself from asking, "What would you do—if it was one of your brothers in jail?"

Scott started to shrug off the question. After all, he knew his brothers, and he knew that none of them would ever end up in the kind of situation Joe Juarez was in. Except he realized that Alicia felt the same way about her brother as he did about his, and that was why she was such a passionate advocate for his cause.

He also knew, from his years on the police force, that human beings were inherently volatile and anyone was capable of almost anything given the right motivation.

Could he imagine LJ smashing the window of an electronics store to lift a new stereo system? Or Ryan going door-to-door to scam people out of their savings in the name of home improvements that would never happen? Or Jake stealing cars to sell on the black market overseas? Of course not—the idea of any of his brothers involved in such criminal activity was ridiculous. On the other hand, he didn't doubt that they were all capable of inflicting serious bodily harm on anyone who threatened someone they cared about.

"I'd do exactly what you're doing," he finally responded to Alicia's question. "And leave no stone unturned in trying to prove his innocence—or at least understand why he'd done whatever it was that landed him in jail."

"Joe didn't take the engine or those plans."

"I know you believe that, and you might be right. But maybe you should think about what circumstances might have forced him into a situation where he decided to take them."

"Joe wouldn't sacrifice his integrity under *any* circumstances."

"What if his integrity demanded he do it?"

"What do you mean?"

"What if he believed the emissions of this alternative fuel were carcinogenic?"

"That isn't what happened here."

"What if something like that did happen?"

"Then he would have urged the company to scrap the project." She handed him a mug of coffee. "Cream? Sugar?"

He shook his head. "No, thanks. And what would Joe do if the company refused?"

She frowned as she sat across from him, obviously considering possibilities she hadn't before and not appreciating the implications. "Can we stick with the facts as they exist?"

"Okay," he said. "What we know is that Joe had taken the prototype and the engine plans home to make some alterations on them over the weekend. On Saturday morning, he couldn't find them.

"According to the statement he later gave to police, he tore the house apart looking for them and, when he still couldn't locate them, put in a call to Gene Russo, his boss. A review of his phone records confirms that the call was made, although he didn't leave a message on Russo's machine."

"Of course he didn't leave a message," she said, a little defensively. "He wanted to talk to his boss in person so he went to track him down—"

"—at the garage," Scott interrupted to continue, reminding her that this was his recitation of facts. "Russo went back to Joe's house with him and they called the police from there."

"And Joe admitted to Mr. Russo and the police that he'd taken the engine and plans home on the weekend, which he wouldn't have done if he'd had something to hide."

That had occurred to him, too. But he'd worked a lot of cases where suspects had unexpectedly admitted to incriminating activities, and he'd found such confessions usually allowed the investigation to be wrapped up quickly. Which is exactly what had happened here.

Had it been wrapped up too quickly?

That was a question he couldn't answer without more information and a close look at the transcripts.

"Other than the fact that Joe was the last person in possession of the items that were stolen, what evidence did the prosecution have?"

"There was a five-thousand-dollar deposit made to Joe's bank account on Friday before the plans went missing."

"*Five* thousand?" It seemed a paltry amount to risk prison for, but he'd known people who did crazier things for less.

"Yes," she said. "And, yes, Joe had unpaid bills."

"What kind of bills?"

"Outstanding medical expenses from Lia's tonsillectomy in the fall."

"How much?"

"He's been making regular payments, but there's still about two thousand owing."

"Anything else?"

"Nothing out of the ordinary. Just the mortgage, household utilities, that kind of thing."

"Credit card bills?"

She shook her head. "He didn't carry a balance on his cards."

"Did he gamble—horses, slots, stock market?"

"No."

"Do drugs?"

Her jaw tightened. "No."

"What did he do?"

"He worked and spent time with his kids."

"Did he have a girlfriend?" he pressed.

"No. He dated occasionally, but no one seriously or exclusively."

"Who else had a key to the house?"

"Me."

"Anyone else?"

"No."

"Not even Joey?"

"No. But he knows there's a spare hidden in the ceramic frog on the back step." She brightened at the implications of that. "Where almost anyone could have found it and come into the house to take the prototype and plans."

"Anyone could have," he agreed. "But there's no evidence that anyone did."

She sighed. "You're right. I'm grasping at straws."

"What did Joe say when the prosecutor asked him about the money?"

Alicia pushed away from the table and went to refill her mug with coffee. "Nothing."

"He didn't answer the question?"

"He didn't testify," she admitted.

"Why not?"

"That seems to be the sixty-four-thousand-dollar question."

Or maybe, Scott couldn't help but think, in this case it was only a five-thousand-dollar question.

Alicia listened to the metal doors clang shut behind her and fought to suppress the instinctive shudder that ran through her every time she heard the sound. She wondered if she'd ever get used to it and desperately hoped not. She didn't want Joe to be stuck in this prison long enough for her to get used to it.

She followed the guard to the visitors' room. It was mostly empty at this time of day, which filled her with both relief and sadness. She felt claustrophobic enough in here without the press of dozens of bodies around her, and yet, she knew that visits from family and friends were the only bright lights these men had, their only connection to the outside world.

She wouldn't have expected to feel any empathy for these convicted criminals, except that her brother was now one of them. He spent his days locked up in this prison with no one for company but the other inmates who lived behind these bars and the guards who monitored their every move.

The thought made her stomach clench. Her brother didn't deserve to be here. And yet, he was here, and she was scared to death that he wouldn't be able to survive without the oppressive environment crushing his spirit.

Joe had always been a kind person, a gentle soul, a dreamer. He believed the best in people and always looked on the bright side, even when life threw him a curveball. And life had thrown him a lot of those, starting with Yvette's unexpected pregnancy when they were both barely out of high school.

Joe had immediately proposed, wanting to marry her and give their baby a family. He hadn't listened to the naysayers who'd warned of the difficult road ahead because he'd believed that their love was strong enough to triumph over whatever obstacles they might face.

And for a while, it looked as though he was right. Joe Jr. was born seven months after they married, then Lia came along four years later. During that time, Joe had worked two and three jobs to provide for his young family. When Yvette started making noises about feeling restless, Joe had done everything he could to make her happy, fought with everything he had to keep their marriage together. In the end, he'd let her go because it was what was best for their children.

Yvette had broken Joe's heart. Alicia knew it because she'd been there for him when his world was falling apart and when he'd started to put it back together again.

She'd been the first person he called when he was hired by Russo's Dirt Devils Racing Team. He'd been as excited as a kid, thrilled with the challenges and opportunities the job would present, and overjoyed to have a steady paycheck that would keep Lia in ballet slippers and allow him to get Joey that computer he'd been eyeing.

He'd worked hard for and with the team. He'd taken pride in their accomplishments while continuing to look ahead at what they could do to perform even better. And he'd been thrilled to be part of their secret project.

There was no way he would have compromised the work. No way he would ever have stolen the prototype or the plans. And she was furious that anyone who knew her brother could even suspect him of such crimes.

The injustice of it all continued to gnaw away at her as she moved over to the table she'd started to think of as her "usual" table and sat in the hard wooden chair waiting for the door at the other end of the room to open.

A few minutes later it finally did, and Joe was led inside.

He looked tired, was her first thought, and thin. He'd lost weight in the few weeks he'd been incarcerated, weight that he couldn't afford to lose from his already slender frame. And the color had faded from his cheeks, leaving his skin pale, almost pasty.

He was little more than a shadow of the vibrant man she loved so dearly, and it broke her heart to see him like this after only five weeks in jail. How could he possibly survive five years?

"Hey, Ali." He managed a smile when she rose to give him a quick hug and a kiss on the cheek before returning to her seat in accordance with the strictly enforced rules of visitation. "I wasn't expecting to see you today."

But she could tell that he was pleased by her visit, grateful for the interruption of his mundane routine.

"I'm on my lunch break so I can't stay long," she told him. "But there was something I wanted to talk to you about."

"Are the kids okay?" he asked, immediately concerned.

"Joey and Lia are fine," she said quickly, anxious to reassure him even while she recognized the falseness of her assurance.

Of course they *weren't* fine—they were going through hell trying to deal with the repercussions of their father being in jail. On the other hand, there wasn't any kind of medical emergency that she suspected Joe was worried about.

"Okay." He exhaled shakily. "Good."

"How about you, Joe?" she asked gently. "Are you okay?"

"Sure," he responded, though not very convincingly.

"I'm worried about you."

"Don't," he said. "Worrying about me in here isn't going to change anything."

"I know," she admitted. "But I can't help it. And I can't help feeling guilty for living my life while yours has been put on hold."

"Joey and Lia are my life, Ali. And because of you, they're able to move on with their lives. I can't tell you how much it means to me that you're there for them."

"It would mean more to them to have their father with them."

He winced as the barb struck home. "Dammit, Ali. You know this wasn't my choice."

"Then why didn't you testify, Joe? Why didn't you take the stand to tell your side of the story?"

"Haven't we been through this already?"

"Not really, because you always refused to answer the question."

"Telling my side of the story wouldn't have changed anything," he told her. "Not without proof that someone else took those plans."

"Then that's what we're going to find."

"What are you talking about?" he asked warily.

"I've hired a private investigator."

"Why?"

She was stunned. "Because you shouldn't be locked up for a crime you didn't commit."

"The jury convicted me," he reminded her.

"Because the jury didn't have all of the evidence."

"Let it go, Ali."

She frowned. "I thought you'd be pleased by this."

"I'll be pleased when my sentence is over and I can be home with my family again."

"Well, hopefully Scott Logan will make that happen sooner rather than later."

"Who?"

"The investigator I hired on the recommendation of your lawyer," she told him.

"Jordan gave you his name?"

She nodded. "Because he believes, as I do, that you were wrongly convicted."

"I can't afford a private investigator," Joe said softly.

"Have I asked you for any money?"

"You can't afford it, either," he reminded her. "You've got your courses to pay for."

As if she could go to medical school while she was working full-time and caring for her brother's children. Maybe becoming a doctor was her lifelong dream, but she could hardly pursue her own self-interests while her family was in such turmoil.

"He wants to meet with you," she said, ignoring his comment.

Joe didn't say anything.

"Which means that you need to put him on your visitor list."

"I don't see what good it will do. I can't tell him anything that I haven't already told you."

"Will you do it anyway?" she asked softly. "Please."

He sighed. "I'll do it, but not because I think he'll actually find anything. Only because you do so much and ask for so little in return."

She managed a smile. "Thank you."

She didn't care about his reasons so long as she got the results she wanted, and she was trusting Scott Logan to get them for her.

Joe felt his cheeks burn with shame as he walked away from the table where Alicia remained sitting. Prison rules required that visitors stay seated while the inmate was returned to his cell. He hated her seeing him like this, locked in a cage, unable to move without a security guard shadowing his every step.

He didn't need to look back to know that she was watching. She had always watched his back, always stood firm in his corner. She wasn't just his sister; she was his unwavering champion, and his closest friend.

And every day since this nightmare had started, he'd thanked God that she was on his side. She was the first person he'd called when he was arrested, the one person he'd always been able to count on, the only person he trusted with the children who owned his heart.

That thought brought a pang, sharp and deep, as did every thought of Joey and Lia.

He'd made his own choices, and he couldn't pretend otherwise. But he'd never imagined that he'd be torn away from them like this, or that every minute away from them would tear him up inside. But even if he'd known then what he knew now, he wouldn't have changed anything. He couldn't.

He'd done what he'd needed to do to protect them. Yet he wasn't naive enough to believe the decisions he'd made would leave them unscathed. They were just children, after all. Children who had lived the last five years without their mother and who now, for all intents and purposes, had lost their father, too.

He worried about Joey, his angry and strong-willed son who was balanced on that shaky precipice between childhood and adulthood, a boy in so many ways, a man in too many others. And Lia, his beautiful little princess and the light of his life, who always led with her heart despite the bruises it suffered too frequently and easily.

He swallowed around the tightness in his throat and stared straight ahead in defiance of the tears that burned his eyes, taking comfort, scant though it was, in the knowledge that his children had Alicia and each other.

Joey and Lia might bicker and fight as siblings tended to do, but they would stand together when it mattered. As he and Alicia had always stood together.

Only now they were standing on opposite sides of a prison wall.

As he waited for the door of his cell to open, he forced that thought from his mind.

Because he knew that Alicia couldn't love Joey and Lia any more if they were her own children and would protect them as if they were her own, he felt some measure of comfort.

He also felt guilt. Because although he'd trusted her with his children, he hadn't trusted her with the one thing she'd been asking for since his arrest.

The truth.

Chapter Four

Scott wasn't the type of man to be preoccupied by thoughts of a woman. But as he made his way toward CRDC through Friday afternoon traffic to visit Joe Juarez, he found himself thinking about Alicia instead of the job she'd hired him to do.

His mind circled back to the one thought that had plagued him throughout the day: he shouldn't have stayed for dinner.

There was a part of him that doubted the wisdom of accepting her as a client, but he knew the real problem was his inability to remember she was a client.

When he'd left the police force and been offered a position at his friend's investigation firm, he'd chosen to specialize in surveillance because it was a job that didn't require much interaction with others and afforded even less opportunity for small talk. In his work, a client was a name on a contract and a corresponding number on a file. A client was not—or at least never had been before—a stunningly attractive woman with fathomless dark eyes, temptingly full lips, shapely mouthwatering curves and the soft and lyrical voice of an angel.

Yeah, dinner had definitely been a mistake.

And then he'd compounded the error by staying to help with dishes and drink coffee. The next thing he knew it was after ten o'clock, Alicia was trying to stifle a yawn, and he was thinking that he needed to go so she could get to bed. Except that thinking about Alicia in bed was another mistake, because he could all too easily picture himself right there with her.

Maybe it wasn't so surprising that he was attracted to her. After all, he was a man and she was…a goddess, he decided, for lack of a better description.

And if he'd met her at a different time and under different circumstances, he might have been tempted to test the attraction he felt, see if it was reciprocated, maybe indulge in the kind of steamy affair Darlene had recommended. But circumstances weren't different, and right now Alicia Juarez probably wasn't looking to further complicate her already complicated life.

Which was a damn shame.

In any event, she'd hired him to do a job and he needed to focus his efforts on doing that job.

But what would happen if he uncovered evidence that incriminated rather than exculpated her brother?

He frowned as he steered into the parking lot of Columbia River Detention Center, certain that such a result would ensure he *never* saw the inside of Alicia's bedroom.

Although he was inclined to believe that Joe Juarez

was somehow involved in the crime of which he'd been convicted, he was keeping an open mind until he had solid evidence that pointed in one direction or the other. In the meantime, he was very interested in hearing what the man himself had to say about the events that had put him behind bars.

He was surprised when the first thing Joe said, after the introductions had been made, was, "You must be well-connected."

"Why do you say that?"

"Because I barely finished filling out the paperwork to add your name to my visitor list, and here you are."

Scott shrugged. "I called the superintendent to inquire if the documentation had been filed and he expedited the process."

"The superintendent?" Joe whistled in mock incredulity.

"Well, I see your son comes by his attitude honestly enough."

The other man's eyes narrowed. "You know Joey?"

"We met last night."

"Ali didn't mention that."

"No?"

Joe just watched him for a long moment before asking, "How do you know Jordan Hall?"

"His sister is married to my cousin."

Joe snorted. "Is that supposed to be a recommendation?"

"Take it any way you want."

"I want to know if you're any good or if my sister wasted her money hiring you."

"Which possibility bothers you more?" Scott asked.

"She wants to be a doctor," Joe said, ignoring the question. "Did you know that?"

"Your sister's plans aren't the reason I'm here."

"Actually they are," Joe countered. "Because she had to have used the money she's been saving for her course fees to pay your retainer."

"Maybe she thought finding the truth about why you're in prison was more important than medical school."

"The truth is that the jury found me guilty," he said bluntly. "And nothing can change that now."

"Alicia is convinced someone set you up."

Joe didn't respond.

"Can you think of anyone who would do that?"

"No."

"Who knew you took the plans home that weekend?"

"Everyone."

"Could you be more specific?"

Joe shrugged. "It wasn't a secret to anyone who worked at Russo's."

"Anyone at Russo's you didn't get along with?"

"I wasn't buddies with everyone, but I'm not going to start pointing fingers at someone else just because we may have had a disagreement at one time or another."

"Someone pointed the finger at you," Scott reminded him.

Again, Joe didn't respond.

"Tell me about the five thousand dollars."

"I didn't know anything about it until after I was arrested."

"According to the bank, it was a cash deposit made at a branch where, coincidentally, there is no video surveillance."

"You've already been in contact with the bank?"

"Just doing my job."

Joe seemed to mull this over.

"The teller who processed the transaction didn't remember very much other than that it was a woman who made the deposit."

"Did she give a description?" Joe asked.

"Nothing except that she was wearing a hat and sunglasses and had the deposit slip already filled out when she got up to the window. She probably would have taken more notice if it was a withdrawal, but deposits aren't usually an issue."

"Yeah, I can't say I'd object to an unexpected cash infusion under different circumstances."

"Can you think of anyone who would have access to that amount of cash and a reason for setting you up?"

Joe shook his head. "No."

"Anyone who knows your bank account number?"

"No," he said again.

Scott sat back in his chair, folded his arms across his chest. "Did you do it?"

"Does it really matter to you whether I did or didn't?" Joe countered.

"Not to me," he admitted easily. "But to your sister and your kids, yeah, it matters. A lot."

"My family's my business."

"You're right. I just thought you'd be a little more cooperative, if for no reason other than concern about what happened the other day."

Joe's eyes narrowed. "What are you talking about?"

"Alicia didn't tell you?"

"Tell me what?" he demanded.

"Somebody slashed the tires on her car."

What little color there'd been in the man's face drained away before he dropped his head into his hands.

"The cops don't know who did it. They think it was a random act of vandalism, but your sister believes differently."

Joe lifted his head again, and Scott knew the fear and helplessness he read in the other man's eyes weren't feigned. "But she's okay. She was here a couple of days ago and she was fine."

"Yeah, she's okay," Scott agreed. "More angry than anything. And convinced that the incident is somehow connected to your being in prison."

"Why—" Joe swallowed. "Why would she think that?"

"Because it happened only a few hours after she'd been to see me, and because the words BACK OFF were written in the dirt on the window."

"What do you think?"

"I'm not a fan of coincidences," he told Alicia's brother. "So I'm not discounting the incident as easily as the police."

"Maybe she should heed that advice."

"Is that what you want her to do—back off?"

"I want her to be safe," Joe said.

Scott knew that, at least, was one hundred percent true.

"Maybe you could tell Ali that you changed your mind or something more urgent came up."

"She'd just hire someone else," Scott pointed out.

Joe sighed. "You're right. Ali doesn't give up on anything."

Scott could tell that he was genuinely worried—

and frustrated that he wasn't in any position to protect his family.

"I can't back off," he said. "But I can keep an eye on your sister and your kids."

Joe considered the offer for a long minute before he nodded. "I don't like owing anyone favors," he admitted. "But I would really appreciate that."

Scott didn't figure it would be much of a hardship to stop by the house every once in a while to check on them. The hard part, he knew, would be keeping his hands off of Alicia.

It had been a hell of a week, Alicia thought to herself as she picked up her study manual and snuck out onto the back porch to steal a few minutes of privacy. The kids were settled down in front of the television with a bowl of popcorn and a favorite movie, and she was anxious to catch up on the reading she'd been neglecting. She settled in her favorite chair close to the light and opened the cover of *Principles of Biochemistry*.

Ten minutes later, she realized she'd read the same paragraph a dozen times without comprehending any of the words.

She'd wanted to be a doctor for as long as she could remember. She loved her job as a nurse and took pride in the work she did at the clinic, but she wanted to do more. And medical school, she knew, was the key.

But how was she ever going to graduate if she couldn't focus?

And how could she even think about medical school when the unity of her family had been shattered?

Yes, she wanted to be a doctor. But right now, what she wanted more than anything else in the world was for her brother to come home.

She tipped her head back and closed her eyes against the wave of emotions that washed over her. Sadness, fear, anger and frustration—all of the feelings so strong and interconnected that she didn't know where one ended and the next began.

There was a lot of anger churning inside her. She was mad at the judge, the jury, the lawyers. She blamed the whole system for this miscarriage of justice. But mostly she was furious with Joe for not fighting.

Because deep in her heart she suspected that Joe held the key to what had happened. She didn't believe for a minute that he was guilty, but she knew that he knew more than he'd told anyone.

The prosecutor had talked about Joe's financial difficulties—the mortgage payments, the medical bills, the usual expenses associated with raising two growing children. But the prosecutor didn't know Joe. She didn't know that he would cut out his own heart before he would steal from someone.

And the jury didn't know, either, because Joe hadn't bothered to testify in his own defense.

Or maybe he'd made the smart choice there, she considered. At least he hadn't screwed up as she had done.

She felt the tide of her anger turn back toward herself as the memories of that day replayed in her mind. She'd been anxious to help, eager to speak on his behalf, desperate for the men and women sitting in judgment to see Joe as he really was.

She'd testified that he was a man devoted to his

family. She'd admitted that nothing was as important to *her* as her family. And when asked if she would do anything for them, she'd answered with an unhesitating "yes," not recognizing the trap that had been set until she saw the prosecutor's slow smile.

"Even lie to keep your brother out of prison?" the A.D.A. queried.

"No!" Alicia shouted.

The judge had sustained Jordan's immediate objection, but Alicia knew the damage had already been done.

Everything she'd told the jury about Joe—his sense of honesty and decency and integrity—had been wiped out by that single question.

And Alicia couldn't really blame the prosecutor for doing her job, for pointing out the truth. Because although she believed with everything in her heart that her brother had not and would not steal those plans, Alicia would protect him even if he had.

She was grateful when she heard the creak of footsteps on the porch, eager for any distraction that would take her mind off of that day. She opened her eyes, expecting to see Lia or Joey. Instead, it was Scott Logan standing in front of her.

Her breath caught in her throat, as it had done the first time she set eyes on him. A purely visceral and entirely female response, and one that she had no intention of revealing to the man with the broad shoulders and bedroom eyes.

"Hi," she said, barely breathing the word into the quiet of the night.

He reached down and picked up the book she'd forgotten was in her lap, his fingertips brushing lightly against her thigh as he did so. She sucked in a quick breath and was thankful he didn't seem to notice.

"Heavy reading," he said, glancing at the title on the cover before he let it drop, with a solid thud, to the floor.

"Too heavy for my current mood," she admitted. "My mind was wandering."

He lowered himself to the floor, leaning his back against the post so that he was facing her. "I see you got your car back."

"Just today," she said. "And though I was glad to have the use of my brother's vehicle while it was in the shop, I'm happy to have it back. It's a lot easier to park in narrow spaces than Joe's truck."

"Speaking of Joe," he said. "I saw him this afternoon."

"You're moving fast."

One corner of his mouth kicked up in a half smile. "I've never had any complaints."

She forced herself to ignore the innuendo and the answering heat that coursed through her veins. "And I'm not complaining," she assured him. "I'm grateful."

"It happens that I don't have a lot of other things on the go right now, and I don't want the evidence in this case to get any colder than it already is."

"Was he any help?"

"Not much," he admitted. "Any idea why he's holding back?"

"No. But I know he didn't sell those plans."

"I think you're right."

"You do?"

He treated her to another one of those quick, fleeting smiles. "Isn't that what you've been trying to convince me of since you first walked into my office?"

"Yes," she admitted.

"So what we need to figure out—"

"We?" she queried.

He shrugged. "You know Joe's habits and routines, his friends and associates. It just seems expedient for us to work together."

"Okay," she agreed, pleased to think that she might be able to help. "Where do we start?"

"With his telephone records," he told her. "I found several calls made to your brother's house, between the time of his arrest and the conclusion of his trial, from a cell phone number that doesn't appear anywhere in his records before or since."

She felt a frisson of excitement skitter down her spine. "Can you track down the owner?"

"I'm trying," he said. "I went to the store where the account was activated, but the customer information they were given seems to be bogus." He pulled a small notebook out of the pocket of his jeans and flipped it open. "The phone was purchased by a woman who gave her name as Elaine Nomolos and an address that apparently doesn't exist."

Disappointment edged out anticipation. "How is that a lead?"

"Because people don't give false names and addresses unless they have something to hide. And because it was a woman who made the five-thousand-dollar deposit into Joe's bank account."

"We're looking for a woman?"

He nodded. "And that's where you come in. I need the names of the women in his life—coworkers, girl-friends, friends."

"I already told you he hasn't been seriously involved with anyone in the past few years."

"I'd say the definition of *serious* is open to interpretation," he countered. "So I'd like the names of everyone he's dated in the past two years."

She thought back, trying to remember. "Staci Lambert...Nadia Wells...Deena McIntyre...Debbie Asher..."

He wrote down each name in a small coil notebook he'd pulled out of his back pocket.

"Those are the only ones I can think of," she said.

"What about the women he works with? Are there any that stand out in your mind?"

"Oh, yeah. He dated Judy Greer casually a few years ago, and they've remained friends."

"A coworker would know he had the plans," Scott agreed. "And have a valid reason to come over to discuss them with him."

"Margo Walsh only started work with the team a few months ago, but I remember Joe mentioning her. They seemed to butt heads on a pretty regular basis, which struck me as unusual because Joe gets along with everyone. Well, almost everyone."

"Almost?"

She shook her head. "Sorry—not anything that can help with the investigation."

"But if Joe made an enemy of someone..."

She shook her head again. "No. He didn't. And Ross certainly didn't think enough of my brother to care..."

"Ross?"

"Harmon," she answered automatically, then scowled

when she saw him writing the name down. "I thought you were looking for a woman."

"The woman could be fronting for someone else," he said. "Tell me about Ross Harmon."

"There's no way he's involved in this."

"How can you be sure?"

"Because his only conflict with Joe was about me."

He lifted an eyebrow.

"I used to…date…Ross."

"And your brother didn't approve?"

"Let's just say the relationship didn't end amicably."

"Because?" he prompted.

"Is this dissection of my private life really necessary?"

"I can't discount Harmon as a suspect unless I know the nature of his conflict with your brother."

"Ross didn't understand why I objected to continuing to sleep with him after he got engaged to someone else. He came by my apartment one day after we'd broken up and my brother was there. Joe told him to leave me the hell alone or he'd need a better doctor than he was to put his vital organs back in the right places." She folded her hands in her lap, stared down at them. "Joe's not a violent person, but he is protective of me."

"When was this?"

"Three and a half years ago." She looked up at him again. "Is that enough information now to convince you to erase his name from your little book and concentrate your efforts elsewhere to find whoever framed my brother?"

Scott hadn't meant to pry into her personal life. Well, not much, anyway. He definitely hadn't intended to dredge up uncomfortable memories. And though he was tempted to apologize, he sensed that would only embarrass her more. Instead, he obliged her by striking a line through the name.

"I'll track down Judy Greer and Margo Walsh," he said, tucking his notebook back in his pocket. "The racing team seems like the most logical place to start."

Before Alicia could respond, the screen door banged open and a four-foot bundle of energy came flying onto the porch.

"*Ice Princess* is finished and now Joey wants to watch the Indy Andy movie on TV but I don't want to because it's scary and then I'll have nightmares." She buried her face in Alicia's shirt.

"Say hello to Mr. Logan," Alicia instructed her niece.

"Hello, Mr. Logan."

"You can call me Scott," he told her, fighting the instinctive wince at hearing the *Mr.* part.

There was a time when he'd been Detective Logan—when that title had made him believe he was someone despite not having a bunch of fancy initials after his name like his father and all of his brothers. But he'd given up the title along with his badge and now he was simply *Mr.* again—the youngest son and biggest disappointment of renowned psychologist and bestselling author, Lawrence Logan.

"There's a boy named Scotty in my class at school," Lia told him. "He picks his nose all the time."

Scott couldn't help but smile at the child's uncensored comment.

"That's not an appropriate topic of conversation,"

Alicia admonished, apparently not so enamored with her niece's guilelessness.

"Well, he does," Lia insisted. "And sometimes he even eats it."

Alicia's face, Scott noticed, was turning an intriguing shade of red.

"I don't doubt it's true," she said. "But it's not really the kind of thing you should talk about in front of company."

"Oh." Her little brow furrowed. "Why not?"

"It just isn't. And anyway, it's time to get you ready for bed."

"But it's Friday and we haven't had ice cream yet and you said you'd paint my toenails."

"That was before you decided you wanted to watch a movie, so you got popcorn instead of ice cream and now it's very late."

Lia looked at her with big brown eyes pleading. "Pleeeaaase. I want my feet to look pretty when I go to Jessica's birthday party tomorrow."

"No one's going to see your toenails through your socks."

"But I want to wear my sandals with my denim skirt and the new pink top you bought for me."

"Honey, it's only May. I'm not sure it will be warm enough for sandals."

"Pleeeaaase," Lia pleaded again.

Alicia sighed as she ruffled the little girl's hair. "Go pick your color."

Lia bounded up, all thoughts of scary movies forgotten in her excitement. "I want Berrylicious and the little flower stickers," she announced, and she raced back inside to find them.

"I don't know what to say," Alicia said, clearly torn between amusement and mortification as the door banged shut—again—behind her niece. "I feel like I should apologize but—"

"Don't," he said. "She's just a little girl saying what's on her mind."

"Yes, that she does."

"I like her," he said, and found himself surprised by how true it was. He didn't have a lot of experience with kids, but there was something about Lia that made it impossible to feel awkward around her. "She's open and honest and unapologetic about it."

"Thank you," she said softly. "So many people make allowances for her because her daddy's in prison—or they blame the fact that her daddy's in prison. They don't really see *her*."

"Then they're the ones who are missing out—she's a great kid."

Alicia's answering smile touched him deep inside, where he hadn't felt anything in a very long time.

"Aunt Alicia." The screen door creaked open, then slapped against its frame a third time as Joey came out onto the porch. "Did you want—oh." He scowled when he saw Scott on the porch. Then, obviously remembering that his aunt would expect him to show better manners, offered a vague, "Hey."

This child, Scott mused, wasn't nearly as open or honest as his sister. But he recognized something of the boy he used to be in the distrustful eyes and insolent attitude of Alicia's nephew and knew that she was going to have her hands full with him.

"Hey," he returned the greeting.

Joey stuffed his hands in the front pockets of his jeans as he shifted his gaze to Alicia. "I just, uh, wondered if you were going to, uh, watch the movie with me."

And though he hadn't accompanied his request with the *pleeeaaase* that his sister used so effectively, Scott knew the request was no less heartfelt.

"I promised Lia that I'd paint her toenails," she said.

"Oh." Joey shrugged. "Yeah, okay, whatever."

Alicia winced, apparently aware that she'd let the boy down, yet unable to break a promise she'd made to one child to appease another. "We could watch it when I'm done."

"It's already started," he said.

"*Raiders of the Lost Ark, Temple of Doom* or *The Last Crusade?*" Scott asked, guessing that the "Indy Andy" movie Lia referred to was one of the Indiana Jones trilogy.

"*Raiders of the Lost Ark.*"

"One of my favorite movies," Scott said.

Joey lifted his head to send him a look that was equal parts suspicion and interest. "You wanna watch it?"

Scott noted the way Alicia's eyes widened—obviously she was as astonished as he was by the invitation.

"Mr. Logan was just leaving." She spoke before he had a chance to respond, before he could get beyond his own surprise to think of a response.

He was grateful for the ready excuse. The last thing he wanted was to hang out with a sullen adolescent when he could be…alone…in his empty apartment. He frowned.

"Oh." The boy dropped his head again.

And Scott found himself thinking that watching TV with the kid couldn't be any worse than watching TV by himself.

"I was going home to turn on the same movie," he said. "But I don't have any popcorn there."

"I'm not sure we have anymore here," Alicia said, clearly keeping open the escape route.

Because she didn't want him to feel obligated to stay?

Or because she wanted him to go?

Maybe he should go. It would probably be a mistake to hang around here with a kid he wasn't even sure he liked and a woman he couldn't deny he was attracted to.

"But we have ice cream," Joey said.

Then again, maybe the kid wasn't so bad.

"What kind?" he asked.

And that was how he ended up eating butterscotch ripple ice cream and watching Indiana Jones with Joey while Alicia went upstairs to paint her niece's toenails.

Almost an hour passed before she returned. She checked the screen, noted that it was a commercial before explaining, "We had to get out her outfit for tomorrow and then make sure her nails were dry before I could tuck her under the covers."

"You missed the part where the guy gets shot and blood comes out of his mouth," Joey said. But there was no censure in his tone, just the typical morbid excitement of a twelve-year-old boy.

"I'm sorry about that," Alicia said dryly.

There was room on the couch, between where Scott and Joey were sitting, but she chose to curl up a chair on the opposite side of the room, tucking her feet beneath her.

"Shh," Joey said, although no one had said anything else. "The movie's coming back on."

Alicia glanced at him over the top of her nephew's head and mouthed, "Thank you."

Scott just shrugged, uncomfortable with her gratitude when he realized he was the one who should be thankful. Because sitting and watching a movie with her nephew was a hell of a lot more fun than sitting alone on a Friday night in front of his own television, as he'd spent too many of his Friday nights lately.

"Oh, gross," Joey said, drawing their focus back to the screen where Indy's girlfriend was attacked by falling skeletons.

Alicia's indrawn breath and closed eyes confirmed that she shared her nephew's assessment of the scene.

The next time he glanced over at her, he saw that her eyes were still closed and that she'd fallen asleep.

"Wasn't that a great movie?" Joey turned to his aunt as the credits started to roll, scowled when he saw that she was sleeping. "I guess she didn't think so."

"I think she was just tired," Scott said.

"Yeah. I guess so." But he was still scowling as he picked up the ice cream bowls off the coffee table. "But she didn't fall asleep painting Lia's toenails, did she?"

"No, I don't think she did."

Joey sighed, as if disappointed that Scott wasn't arguing with him. "I know it's been an adjustment for her, too, to go from being a single career woman to full-time guardian of two busy kids. At least that's what Mrs. H. said."

"That's probably true," Scott said. "And though I don't know your aunt very well, I do know there isn't anywhere she'd rather be than here with you and your sister."

"Yeah. I guess so," the boy said again. Then, "Do you think I should wake her?"

"No," Scott decided. There were still more things

he'd hoped to talk to her about tonight, but it wasn't anything that couldn't wait. "Let her sleep. You can lock the door behind me."

"Okay." Joey carried the bowls into the kitchen.

Scott hesitated a minute before pulling a knitted afghan off the back of the sofa. She sighed softly when he tucked it around her, then snuggled deeper into the chair.

"Sweet dreams," he murmured.

Chapter Five

Alicia woke with a start and winced at the bright sunlight streaming through the bedroom window. Then she realized she wasn't in her bedroom but in the living room, where she'd obviously fallen asleep watching the movie last night. While Scott Logan was there.

She felt her cheeks heat, embarrassed by the realization she'd flaked out in front of company.

And not just any company, but a man who made her heart pound just a little bit harder and her blood flow a little bit faster. Although last night, apparently, she'd felt comfortable enough in his presence to close her eyes and fall asleep. Or maybe she'd just been exhausted.

She tucked her knees up to her chest and wrapped the blanket around them.

Blanket?

She didn't remember taking the blanket off the sofa.

In fact, she was certain she hadn't. She was equally certain that Joey wouldn't have thought to cover her up with it. Which left only one other explanation—Scott Logan.

Her embarrassment moved into the realm of mortification.

And yet, at the same time, an unexpected feeling of warmth coursed through her.

She couldn't remember the last time anyone had tucked her in and could only guess that it had been her mother when she was probably about Lia's age. Now she was a thirty-year-old woman, and well past the age when she'd expected to be tucking her own children into bed at night. But she had Joey and Lia now, and no time to be fantasizing about tucking herself under the covers with a handsome P.I. just because he stirred feelings inside her that had long been dormant.

It was one thing to be attracted to the man. After all, he was the embodiment of tall, dark and handsome and she was a woman with blood flowing through her veins. But it was something else entirely—and far more dangerous to her peace of mind—to imagine that she could actually start to like him.

And what woman wouldn't like a man who actually paid attention to the children in her care? Who anticipated and responded to their needs? Who anticipated and responded to her own needs—even if it was only for a decent night's sleep?

Yeah, maybe she was starting to like him, and the liking was starting to weaken the shields around her heart just a little. Because it was more than just his good looks, muscular arms and broad shoulders that appealed to her. It was the kindness of his soul and generosity of spirit that made her think he was the type of man heroes were made of, the type of man her heart secretly yearned for and the type of man she'd given up hope of ever meeting.

No, that was ridiculous. He was just a man, and she wasn't looking for a hero.

The pounding of feet on the stairs—no gentle pitter-patter from her brother's children—reminded her that breakfast was a more immediate concern than her wayward fantasies.

As she untangled herself from the chair, she decided she'd make pancakes. It was a favorite comfort food of her own childhood and a substantial breakfast that she hoped would give them solace and strength for the task ahead: visiting their father in prison.

Whether he was in the office or out on a case, Scott didn't think twice about working weekends. One day—whether it was a Sunday or a Wednesday or any other—was pretty much the same as the one that came before and the one that would come next. If there was work to be done, he'd go into the office to do it. If there wasn't, he'd take some time off.

Today, he was working on the Juarez case, thinking about Alicia's dream to be a doctor and the fact that she was using money she'd saved for medical school to hire him. It shouldn't matter to him, but it did.

Maybe that was why he was in his office doing background work that could have waited until Monday—because it was easier to justify not billing hours that no one but himself knew he'd put in.

Not that Trevor would say anything about it. Scott earned enough money for the firm that his boss wouldn't complain about a little bit of pro bono work, but he wasn't prepared to answer questions about his reasons for cutting costs on this case. And he was sure if Trevor got a look at Alicia, he'd assume that Scott was sleeping with her—or at least wanted to. And though he could deny the sleeping part, he couldn't deny the wanting.

And he cursed himself for ever signing her on as a client.

Then again, their professional relationship was only one of the many reasons he knew he couldn't get involved with a woman like Alicia. A bigger reason—or rather, two bigger reasons—were the children in her care.

Not that he had anything against kids, and not that Joey and Lia were bad kids, it was just that kids required a commitment, and he didn't do commitments.

Not since his live-in girlfriend of almost four years walked out on him more than two years earlier.

Of course, his whole life had started to nose-dive like a sinking ship when his partner was killed, so he couldn't really blame her for bailing out when she did. And when his friend Trevor offered him a job at his investigation agency, Scott was ready to reach for the lifeline it was.

In the two years since, he'd preferred to work behind the scenes and keep his interaction with clients to a minimum. At least until Alicia Juarez walked into his office.

Four days later, he still couldn't stop thinking about her. He was letting this case become personal, and though he knew that was a mistake, he wanted to help her. He wanted to give her the results she wanted, to prove that her confidence in him wasn't misplaced.

He glanced up at the knock, surprised to realize he hadn't heard the outside door open, even more surprised to see Alicia and her nephew standing in the hall.

"Sorry to interrupt," she said. "But we just dropped Lia off at her ballet class and Joey wanted to stop by. He said you said it was okay for him to come in and see your office."

"Of course it's okay," he said.

"Hey, cool," Joey said, making a beeline for the dartboard he'd spotted on the far wall.

"Joey—" Alicia started to protest.

"He's fine," Scott said.

She still looked uncertain as she watched her nephew remove the darts from the board, so Scott took her arm to steer her out of the room where she wouldn't be able to see—and therefore worry.

"How about a cup of coffee?" he offered. "Caroline doesn't come in on weekends, so it's safe for me to touch the coffeemaker as long as I make sure it's clean before I leave. In fact, I just put on a fresh pot a few minutes ago."

"Coffee sounds great." But she sent a last nervous glance over her shoulder as they moved down the hall.

He led the way into the small kitchenette and pulled two mugs from the counter.

"I didn't notice the dartboard when I was here the other day," Alicia said.

Scott shrugged. "You're not a twelve-year-old boy."

"No, I'm not," she agreed. "And neither are you."

He poured her a mug of coffee, black, and handed it to her, before filling his own.

"Thanks." She sipped, then sighed. "Oh, this is good. And I really needed the jolt of caffeine."

"Didn't sleep well?"

Her cheeks flushed. "I slept very well," she said. "So I guess I should thank you for that—for the blanket."

"My pleasure."

The color in her cheeks deepened just a little. "I also wanted to thank you for hanging around last night. It's hard, sometimes, trying to balance the needs of both kids, and I'm sure there were things you would rather have been doing than watching television with a surly preteen boy, but I wanted you to know that I appreciated it. And I know it meant a lot to Joey to have some company."

"What about your needs?" he asked.

She choked on her coffee, which made him want to smile. If he'd had any doubts that Alicia was feeling the attraction that tugged at him whenever they were in the same room together, her reaction to his question effectively eliminated them.

"Excuse me?" she managed to ask after she'd finished coughing and sputtering.

"You mentioned the difficulty of balancing their needs," he said, pretending that his mind hadn't gone straight down the same path as hers and that he wasn't gratified by her response. "And you're obviously doing everything you can to help the kids adjust, but what about you?"

"I'm the adult," she reminded him. "It's my job to take care of them."

There was a thump, then another, and her eyes grew wide. She quickly set her mug onto the counter and turned to leave, clearly wanting to stop Joey from whatever havoc he was wreaking.

He caught her wrist in his hand, halting her retreat

before she'd taken the first step. "It's okay," he said. "He's moved from darts to basketball now."

"You have a basketball net in your office?" She pulled her arm out of his grasp, but not before he'd registered the skip of her pulse.

He shrugged again. "It helps combat the boredom of slow days. But we were talking about you. What have you done for yourself lately?"

"I slept in until eight o'clock this morning."

"That isn't quite what I meant."

Now she shrugged. "Between work and the kids' extracurricular activities, there isn't a lot of time for personal indulgences."

"And if there was?"

"I'd have someone else paint my toenails," she said, a little wistfully.

He had to smile at that. "You're a wild woman, Miss Juarez."

She laughed. "Well, you asked."

"Yes, I did," he agreed, starting back to his office as an idea began to form in his mind. "How long is Lia going to be at ballet?"

"Why?" she asked, stepping ahead of him through the doorway.

He reached up to intercept the ball that Joey sent arcing toward the basket just as Alicia stepped into its path.

"Good save," Joey muttered.

Scott tossed the ball back to him as Alicia continued into the room, apparently oblivious to how close she'd come to wearing the coffee she carried.

"When does your sister's ballet class finish?" he asked Joey.

"Four o'clock," the boy answered. "But she's going from there to a birthday party, so we don't have to pick her up until seven."

"What do you think, Joe—are you game for hanging out with me until then?"

"Sure," the boy agreed readily.

Alicia began to protest. "I couldn't ask—"

"You didn't ask," he reminded her. "I'm offering."

"Why?" she asked.

"Because I need you to do me a favor."

Her eyes narrowed suspiciously. "What kind of favor?"

"Just let me make a phone call," he said. "Then I'll let Aster fill you in on all the details."

Alicia stood on the sidewalk and stared at the pink and green neon letters that spelled out Just Chillin' Salon & Spa. She didn't know how this was doing a favor for Scott, but he'd been so earnest and persuasive, she'd been unable to refuse. And really—what woman in her right mind would turn down a spa day?

Then again, she'd never seen anything like Just Chillin' and though she knew Aster was expecting her, she hesitated.

Before she had decided whether to advance or retreat, the door was pushed open from the inside and a woman with electric blue hair stepped out. Her eyes were heavily lined with black pencil, the lids covered in something that was sparkly and pink, and her lips were painted purple. She wore skintight pink capris and a white T-shirt that had a pair of sparkly pink lips at the center.

"She's a colorful character," Scott had warned, the corners of his mouth curving ever so slightly in that intriguing half smile that created flutters in her belly and made her wonder—and worry—at the effect it would have if he ever really smiled at her. "But she'll take good care of you, I promise."

Alicia guessed this was the colorful Aster, and she was suddenly certain that she didn't want this woman taking care of her.

"Come in, come in," Aster said, pulling her through the door. "Scott called just as I was about to close up for the day, so that was lucky, wasn't it?"

"Oh, if you were ready to go home, I don't want to—"

"I never turn away a client," Aster said. "Especially on the recommendation of a friend."

"But—"

"And Scott said you had somewhere to be at seven," Aster rambled right over Alicia's weak protest, "so we shouldn't waste any more time gabbin'."

"Really, I'm not sure—"

"Don't be nervous, honey. You're in good hands with me. 'Course, you'd probably rather be in the hunky P.I.'s hands than my own—" she gave an exaggerated wink "—and I can't say as I'd blame you on that one, but I promise you, I know what I'm doin' here."

Alicia felt her cheeks flood with color. "I'm afraid you've misinterpreted my relationship with Mr. Logan."

Aster's smile only widened. "I don't think so, honey. A man calls up askin' me to give a woman a special treatment, there's only one interpretation to give it."

Alicia wanted to protest further but decided it might be wiser to just let the subject drop. Which, of course, only gave Aster the opportunity to expound on her theory.

"And about time, I say. That man's been alone long enough. Not that anyone could blame him for being wary after the way his ex ran out on him."

"Ex?" she asked, unable to help herself.

"Girlfriend, not wife," Aster supplied helpfully. "As far as I know, he's never been married. Hasn't even dated seriously, in fact, since Janie left him, and that was more than two years ago.

"And a man as hunky and good-lookin' as Scott Logan—well, people start to wonder if he goes too long without a steady woman in his life. People start thinkin' he's battin' for the other team all of a sudden.

"So I was more than pleased when he called to say you'd be comin' by. And I have to say, a woman like you would nip any of that kind of gossip in the bud.

"Not that he was gossipin'," Aster continued as she led the way through the main salon and down the hall to a private room. "Because he would never do any such thing and would certainly never violate a client's confidence, but he did say that your life had been turned upside down recently and that you were in need of some pamperin'.

"So—" she gestured to a chair "—that's what we're goin' to do."

Alicia sat as directed and Aster crossed the room to a minifridge and pulled out a bottle of wine. She filled a crystal glass with pale straw-colored liquid and brought it to Alicia.

"It's a pinot grigio from Italy," she said.

Alicia took the glass automatically and then sipped because it seemed the polite thing to do. And maybe a glass of wine would help her loosen up a little, reduce her apprehension about putting herself in the hands of the woman with the very blue hair.

"We'll start with a manicure and pedicure," Aster said, bringing over a tub filled with warm water that she set beneath Alicia's chair. "Just slip off your shoes and slide your feet in there."

Alicia smiled as she did so. Maybe a pedicure didn't make her a wild woman, but it sure made her happy.

"You're a nurse, aren't you?" Aster said, then continued on without waiting for a response. "Nurses spend a lot of time on their feet, so takin' care of them shouldn't be a luxury but a necessity."

"How did you know I was a nurse?"

"I saw you wearin' your scrubs the other day when you were waitin' outside Mr. Logan's office."

"I didn't see you," Alicia said, certain she would have remembered.

"I had just scooted into the diner down the street for my breakfast, and you looked a little preoccupied. Whatever it was that turned your life upside down must have been weighin' heavily on your mind."

"It was," Alicia agreed and took another sip of her wine. "And is."

"Anythin' you want to talk about?"

Alicia started to shake her head, then reconsidered.

In the past few months, there hadn't been anyone—other than her friend Sarajane Gerrity, of course—who she felt comfortable enough with to talk about everything that had happened. Now her best friend was busy building her life with Jordan Hall, and though Alicia was thrilled for her, she missed talking to her the way they used to. And suddenly it didn't seem so weird to unload her baggage on this complete stranger who had kind, understanding eyes beneath the sparkly pink shadow.

So she took another sip of wine, then said, "My brother's in prison."

And as Aster worked on her hands and her feet, Alicia found herself pouring out the story.

When her glass was empty, Aster silently refilled it. It occurred to Alicia that maybe she should decline—she really wasn't much of a drinker. But the cool wine was quite tasty and she was definitely starting to feel more relaxed, so she accepted the second glass without protest.

When she'd finished her story—and the second glass of wine—Aster had her strip out of her clothes for a massage.

"Well, if anyone can find out the truth about what happened to your brother, it's Scott," Aster told her as she kneaded the tight muscles of her shoulders. "He used to be a cop, you know."

"Joe's lawyer, Jordan Hall, mentioned that."

"Jordan's sister, Jenny, was my lawyer," Aster said, "when I finally left the no-good bastard I was dumb enough to marry.

"That's how I met Scott," she admitted. "I was in the hospital for the third time that year. I don't remember what it was that time—my excuse, I mean. Whether I'd fallen down the stairs, walked into a wall, tripped over the rug. But it was one of the usual stories women make up to deny that their husbands are usin' them as punchin' bags.

"Of course, the doctors know it, and they're required by law to call the police. And the police come, but unless the victim—God, I hate that word, hate knowin' I was a victim. Anyway, unless the victim is willin' to press charges, nothin' ever happens.

"But this was the second time that Scott responded to the call. And he sat beside my bed in the emergency room, looked me point-blank in the eye and said, 'You know he isn't goin' to change, Aster, and if you stay with him, your life isn't goin' to get any better.'

"And somewhere deep inside, I knew that he was right. But I was more afraid of my life without Nathan—that was my husband—than the beatings. And besides, Nathan was always so apologetic afterward, so sorry for losin' his temper. And when I said this to Scott, he said, 'I'm sure he is sorry. And I'm sure he's goin' to be equally sorry when he finally kills you. But no matter how remorseful he is, you'll still be dead.'

"And maybe his words were harsh, but they were exactly what I needed to make the decision to get out. And he came back the next day, when I was released from the hospital, and drove me to the women's shelter.

"He wasn't just a good cop," Aster said. "He was a real-life hero who actually cared about the people he served, who really believed he could and wanted to make a difference.

"Of course, all that changed when Freddie was killed." She paused long enough to release a heartfelt sigh. "You know about Freddie?"

"I don't think so."

"Freddie Juleson. He was Scott's partner and best friend—until he was gunned down right in front of him. He died in Scott's arms."

Alicia winced instinctively.

"Somethin' like that changes a person. No way

around it. And then, to top it off, his girlfriend up and left him. She couldn't handle the changes—although I don't think she ever really tried. She was too busy buildin' her own career to worry that his whole life was fallin' apart."

"But as a cop, he must have understood the risks of the job," she said.

"Sure he did," Aster agreed. "And he was willin' to take those risks because he believed in the system. But when Freddie's killer got off, Scott lost faith. That's when he handed in his badge and gun and walked away from the job."

"I can't imagine how a person ever gets over something like that," Alicia murmured.

"A person never does," Aster told her. "They just go on. Of course, you probably think I just keep goin' on— and you'd be right. I do like to talk, but I shouldn't've picked such a depressing topic when I'm tryin' to get you to loosen up."

"I'm feelin' pretty loose," Alicia admitted.

"That's the lavender—it's the best I know for takin' care of the knots and kinks in your system. Although I have to admit, your system had more knots and kinks than any I've had my hands on in a long time."

"Well, your hands are the best I've had on my system in a very long time," Alicia told her.

Aster hooted with laughter. "Honey, I'm as flattered as I am sure that won't be true for very much longer. Now get your clothes back on and your butt into that other chair so I can work some more magic."

"What kind of magic?"

"A haircut—just a trim," she amended quickly.

"Maybe a few streaks and a little makeup to highlight your already stunning features."

"I'm not sure," Alicia hedged, and Aster looked so disappointed she immediately felt guilty. "It's not that I don't trust you, it's just that I can't really afford—"

"Honey, none of this is costing you a dime," Aster promised.

"But that isn't right—"

"I told you how it is that I know Scott," Aster reminded her. "So you know that I owe him my life. I've been after him for years to come in and try out some of the salon services. Of course, bein' a man's man, he won't step foot inside this place. If you let me do this for you, it will at least be a small payment on that debt I owe to him."

Alicia sighed. "Put like that, how can I refuse?"

Chapter Six

Scott let Joey get his fill of darts and basketball and the games on his computer before he took the kid into Trevor's office to show him something different.

"A pinball machine?" Joey's eyes practically bugged out of his head.

"Pretty cool, huh?"

"Wow." The boy stared at the machine with something akin to reverence. Then his eyes narrowed on Scott. "How come you've got so many neat things in your office?"

"This is actually Trevor's office," he admitted. "But in exchange for letting him play darts or shoot baskets, he lets me play pinball."

"But aren't you supposed to, like, work?"

Scott smiled at that. "Yeah, but my boss believes that people work harder if they're given the chance to play.

And it's amazing how much tension you can release zinging a little ball around some bumpers."

"I used to think my dad had the coolest job in the world," Joey said softly.

"I imagine a lot of guys would trade in their suits and six-figure salaries to do what your dad does."

"What he *did*," the boy corrected harshly. "He doesn't got a job anymore."

He could hear the anger and frustration in the boy's voice, and though his only experience with adolescent boys was the one he'd been, he sensed that this was Joey's way of reaching out for someone to talk to. And with his dad in jail and his aunt at the spa, Scott was the kid's only choice. "I guess you're pretty mad at your dad, huh?"

Joey snorted. "You mean because he got himself sent to prison after promising he wouldn't walk out like our mom did?"

Scott plugged the coins into the machine, thinking that zinging the ball around might help the kid work out some of his frustrations. He gestured for Joey to go ahead. The kid stepped up to the machine, grasping the edges with his thumbs on the buttons like a pro.

"Where's your mom now?" Scott asked, not certain it was a safer topic of conversation but undeniably curious. Alicia hadn't said much about her brother's ex-wife and Joe hadn't mentioned her at all, leading Scott to assume that she was out of the picture. But maybe he'd been wrong.

The kid shrugged as bells dinged and lights flashed. "Probably getting high somewhere."

"Your mother's a drug addict?"

"And a whore."

He didn't know if he was more shocked by the word the kid used or the matter-of-fact tone with which he said it.

"That's why my dad got custody," Joey continued, scowling as he pulled back the trigger to launch his second ball after the first dropped out of play. "Even though my mom told the judge Lia wasn't his."

"How do you know that?" he couldn't help but ask.

"People talk."

Scott knew through firsthand experience that was true. Whether truth or lies or innuendo, there were always people who would talk. And kids could be crueler than adults, wielding words like weapons, striking out with names and labels they might not even understand except in the context of the damage they could do.

He could imagine the torment Joey endured in the playground every day, taunts about his crack addict mother and convict father. The kid was carrying far more baggage than anyone his age should ever have to handle.

"Do you see your mom very often?" he asked.

"Maybe once a year." A quick grin flashed across the boy's face as the ball zipped back and forth between two pillars and the numbers that indicated his score zipped ever higher. "It's usually around Christmas that she shows up, asking him for money so she can buy us a gift. And my dad gives it to her, thinking that maybe she'll actually follow through."

"Has she been around since your dad went to jail?" Scott hoped not, but he couldn't help but think that it would be an opportune time, from the mother's perspective, to reassert her parental rights.

"Only once," the kid said. "But Aunt Alicia sent her away."

There was so much more he wanted to know, but he didn't want to drag the answers from this boy who was already dealing with so much.

"You going to let me play anytime soon?" he asked instead.

"I've still got one more ball after this," Joey told him.

"I know," Scott said, impressed by the skill with which the boy handled the machine. "Where did you learn to play like that, anyway?"

"There's a little pizza place near the school," he said. "Me and some buddies go over at lunch sometimes to play."

"You got the top score?"

"Yeah." Joey grinned again as more lights flashed and his score continued to climb. "So, are you dating Aunt Alicia or what?"

"Dating?" After the other things that had come out of the kid's mouth, maybe he shouldn't have been surprised by the question. But he was—and he was wary. "Of course not. Why would you think something like that?"

"Because of the way you look at her."

Either the boy was a lot more observant than Scott had given him credit for, or he was more smitten with the beautiful nurse than he'd realized.

"Your aunt and I are not dating," he said again.

"Why not?" Joey asked. "Don't you think she's pretty?"

"Yes, but—"

"She's smart, too," Joey cut in. "And she's going to be a doctor someday."

"Yeah, I heard that."

"So why don't you want to date her?"

"Maybe she doesn't want to date me," Scott suggested, trying to figure out how their conversation had taken this unexpected turn—and how he might redirect it again.

"I think she'd say yes if you asked her out."

The idea had crossed his mind without the kid's interference. Of course, he'd immediately discarded the idea, for a lot of reasons, but now he found himself reconsidering.

"What makes you think so?" he asked, feeling only slightly guilty about pumping Alicia's nephew for inside information about her personal life.

"Because she looks at you the same way you look at her." The second ball fell out of play and he swore softly.

Scott figured Alicia might chastise him for the inappropriate language, but it wasn't his place to do so.

"You could take her to a movie," Joey said as he sent his last ball spinning through the maze of bumpers. "She likes action flicks and science fiction."

"Really?"

"She likes mushy girl movies, too," the boy confided. "But she usually cries during those."

That didn't surprise him at all. "Does she go out to the movies very often?"

Joey flipped the ball to the top of the course again. "Nah. She hasn't really dated anyone since the doctor."

Dr. Ross Harmon, he remembered, and wondered what a woman like Alicia had ever seen in a man like the one she'd described to him. Then again, he was a doctor—as she hoped to be one day herself. Maybe it wasn't so unlikely that she'd been attracted to Harmon.

Maybe it was more unlikely to think that she was attracted to him.

And yet, there was no denying that the air sizzled whenever they were in close proximity. And whenever he touched her—whether the contact was deliberate or inadvertent—there were definite sparks.

"And she's thirty now," Joey continued. "Too old to be choosy if she plans to get married and have kids of her own."

And that quickly, Scott's fantasy evaporated.

Not because of the revelation of Alicia's age, but because Joey was right about his aunt being the type of woman who would want to marry and have children. And while the idea of family used to hold a certain appeal, it wasn't the kind of life he could imagine for himself. Not anymore.

"Your turn," Joey finally said, stepping away from the pinball machine.

Scott shook his head at the score the kid had racked up. "What's the point? There's no way I can beat you."

The kid grinned, then his gaze focused on something behind Scott and his eyes slowly widened. "Wow."

He turned to see what had caught the boy's attention and found himself equally captivated by the woman in the doorway.

He's sent Alicia to Aster's salon in the hopes that a few hours of pampering would help relax her. He hadn't expected a complete makeover, but couldn't deny the transformation was stunning.

Her hair, tied back in a ponytail when she'd shown up at his office earlier that morning, now framed her face in long layers. Her lips had been painted a glossy pink color, her cheekbones highlighted with powder, and her eyes lined and shadowed in a way that made them seem even darker and bigger.

"Wow," he echoed Joey's word softly.

"You look nice, Aunt Alicia."

She gave her nephew a shy smile. "Thanks."

Scott didn't think *nice* was quite the right word. *Wow* was definitely more appropriate.

"Has he been good?" Alicia asked.

"Yeah," he managed, still drinking in the sight of her like a dehydrated marathon runner eyeing the water station across the finish line.

"Are you gonna play?" Joey asked, his voice tinged with impatience.

"You play for me," Scott told him, slowing moving across the room toward Alicia.

"Cool," came the response, before the pinball machine started to whir and ding again.

"Aster promised she wouldn't make my hair blue," Alicia said, gesturing to the subtle gold and auburn highlights that had been added to her dark hair. "But this is still a radical change for me."

"I like it," he told her.

She tucked a strand behind her ear. "I usually have it all one length, it makes it easy to braid or throw into a ponytail. But Aster said the layers would add body and help frame my face."

"She did a good job. You look…incredible. And very relaxed."

Her lips curved in a smile so radiant and stunning it took his breath away.

"She painted my toenails orange."

"You had a successful day, then," he guessed.

She nodded. "And I had a massage. Aster gives an incredible massage—she rubbed this scented oil all over my body…"

Scott tuned her out. It was a matter of self-preservation because the mental image of Alicia's naked body covered in oil was simply too much for him to handle with her nephew playing pinball ten feet away.

"…then there was the wine."

"Wine?" Scott asked, trusting that it was now safe to tune back in to the conversation.

"I had three glasses of wine," she admitted in a whisper.

Which probably explained the sparkle in her eye.

He glanced at the clock, noted that she'd been gone almost four hours. She probably wasn't over the legal limit, but she was definitely impaired. "Not usually much of a drinker?"

She shook her head. "I always stop with two glasses. Any more than that and my head starts to spin and my body starts to tingle."

Hell, if that didn't conjure up all kinds of interesting images in his mind.

He swallowed and took a strategic step back, reminding himself that she was impaired and that her nephew was in the room. "Is your head spinning now?"

"Just a little."

"Then it might be a good idea for me to drive you home," he said.

Not only did Scott drive them home, he stopped at a neighborhood Thai restaurant on the way so that Alicia wouldn't have to cook dinner.

"I feel as if I've been completely spoiled today," she admitted as she unpacked the bag of food.

"You deserved a break," Scott said. "Plus, I figured that if I bought dinner, I could stay to eat and not feel guilty about poaching another meal."

"I usually cook more than enough food, so company is always welcome."

"You shouldn't say that to a man whose entire grocery cart is usually filled with microwaveable dinners." He popped a deep-fried wonton into his mouth, chewed.

She smiled. "I wouldn't say it if I didn't mean it."

"And what if I stopped by unexpectedly one night while you were…entertaining?"

"Entertaining?" she echoed, amused. "If you're talking about book club meetings or weekly cocktail parties, don't worry. I don't have time for anything like that."

"Actually, I meant dating."

She shook her head. "I don't have time for that, either. And even if I did, dating just isn't one of my priorities right now."

"Because of the kids?" he guessed.

"They've been through a lot recently, and they need to know that they can count on me to be there for them."

"Where does their mother fit into the picture?"

"She doesn't. I told you that the other day."

"Yeah, but you didn't tell me she was a drug addict."

"Who did?"

"Joey."

She frowned. "You asked Joey about his mother?"

"I didn't pump the kid for information while you were being buffed and polished at Aster's, if that's what you're thinking," he assured her. "We were just talking and he mentioned that she'd walked out on them."

"Actually Joe kicked her out." Alicia dropped her voice so the kids in the other room wouldn't overhear. "When he realized she was too doped up most of the time to take care of her own children."

"She doesn't see them?"

"Hardly ever." She opened the drawer to get out serving spoons, then called Lia to set the table, effectively terminating that topic of conversation—at least for the moment.

He had more questions about Joe's ex-wife, questions that needed to be answered, but those would have to wait until after dinner, when he could talk to her without risk of the kids overhearing.

Joey followed his sister into the kitchen. "Is it time to eat yet? I'm starving."

"In a minute," Alicia told him.

"Good." He sat in his usual spot while Lia walked around, carefully folding and then setting a paper napkin at each place. Then she circled the table again, placing a fork on top of each napkin. Joey swung his feet under the chair, rhythmically thumping the table leg, and Alicia felt the gentle wine-induced hum inside her head become a swarming buzz.

"Why don't you help your sister?" Scott suggested.

Joey scowled. "Because it's her job to set the table and my job to clear it."

"But if you worked together," he pointed out, "both jobs would get done a lot faster."

Joey considered that for a moment, and while he did, the thumping stopped. Then he grumbled, "All right," and pushed his chair back.

"Anything I can do to help?" Scott asked her.

"You already have—more than you know." She smiled. "But if you want, you can give me a hand to get this food on the table."

Dinner was a relatively quiet event. Possibly because Joey was so hungry, he spent more time chewing than talking. Of course, Alicia immediately felt guilty for the uncharitable thought even while she acknowledged that the peacefulness wouldn't last.

She knew that Joey and Lia weren't unlike Joe and herself at similar ages. They used to fight like cats and dogs, and yet they were always there for one another. She took comfort in that memory, trusting that as much as Joey picked on his sister and Lia tormented her brother, they at least had each other.

She glanced up from her own meal when she saw her nephew stretching his arm out across table.

"Don't reach, Joey," Alicia said.

"But I want the milk."

"Then ask your sister to pass it."

The boy gave a long-suffering sigh. "Pass the milk, Lia."

Now it was her turn to sigh. "How about—Lia, can you please pass the milk?"

The little girl dutifully picked up the milk pitcher and handed it to her brother while she announced, "I'm not Lia—I'm Ail Zerauj."

Joey snorted. "Where'd you come up with a stupid name like that?"

"It's not stupid," his sister said, folding her arms across her chest and glaring at him. "It's my new secret identity."

"Secret identity." Joey snorted again.

"Joey," Alicia warned.

"How did you come up with that one?" Scott asked, stepping in to defuse their argument before it escalated further.

"We played a game at Jessica's birthday party where we figured out what our names were if they were spelled backwards," she told him.

"Anna Noonan was Anna Nanoon, and Jessica's mom said that was because her name was a pal—and—" Her brow wrinkled as she tried to remember.

"Palindrome," Alicia said. "It's a word that's spelled the same way forward and backward."

Lia nodded. "But my name was Ail Zerauj."

"I remember doing the same thing as a kid," Scott said. "I was Ttocs Nagol, and even though I was the youngest, I got to be leader of the Nagol clan because my name was much cooler than Ecnerwal, Nayr or Ekaj."

"Ecnerwal?" Lia wrinkled her nose in distaste.

Scott laughed. "Exactly."

"Can I have another spring roll, Yeoj?" Alicia asked.

Joey was still scowling, as if undecided whether the name game was fun or dumb, and it took him a minute to realize he was being addressed. "Oh," he finally said, and smiled a little as he passed her the box.

"Let's take a walk," Scott suggested after dinner was over and dishes put away.

"Let me just make sure the kids are settled." She ducked upstairs for a moment. "They're in their rooms—Joey with his headphones on and his music blaring, and Lia in bed with a book."

"You're okay with going out for a bit?"

"As long as we don't go far."

"Just down the street a little way," he suggested.

"Okay." She followed him outside, locked the door behind her. "Did I thank you for today?"

He smiled. "Only about half a dozen times."

"I told you—alcohol makes my head spin."

"And your body tingle."

Her cheeks flushed. "I can't believe I actually told you that."

"Makes me wonder what other secrets I might have got out of you if you'd had a fourth glass."

"A fourth glass would have probably rendered me completely incoherent."

"Might have been interesting anyway."

She laughed. "Probably not. And getting back to what I was saying—I wanted to add another thank-you to the list."

"For?"

"Being so great with the kids. I couldn't possibly love them any more than I do, but even I know they're not always easy. And lately—" She shook her head. "Sorry. I'm sure there was a reason you wanted to walk, and it wasn't just to listen to me talk."

"I like listening to you talk," he said. "And I don't mind if there's something you need to vent about."

"There is," she admitted. "I had a parent-teacher conference at Joey's school last week."

"Obviously it didn't go well."

She shook her head. "His teacher says he's uncommunicative and uncooperative, the work he does in class is substandard, and he failed a recent math test because he handed it in without any of the questions answered."

"And what did the teacher suggest you should do?"

"Apparently it's not the teacher's job to actually help solve the problem, only to make sure that I'm aware of it."

"I'd think the problem's pretty obvious," Scott said. "The kid's life has been turned upside down, he's angry and upset and acting out."

"But what's the solution?" she asked wearily. "I've replaced medical texts with parenting books, but there's so much contradictory advice. And, of course, nothing I've found deals specifically with helping a child cope while his father's in prison."

"They got a raw deal, no doubt about that. And I'm sure you're feeling as helpless and frustrated as they are," he said. "But from what I've seen, you're doing a great job."

"Yeah, that's why Joey's uncommunicative and uncooperative."

"Most preteen boys are uncommunicative and uncooperative," he told her. "And I promise, it will get worse before it gets better."

"Great—something to look forward to. And how am I supposed to brainstorm conflict resolution with a kid who won't communicate with me?"

"Brainstorm conflict resolution," he repeated, wondering why that particular phrase sounded so familiar. Then his lips started to curve. *The Most Important Thing?*"

"You've read it?"

"I've lived it," he told her. "Lawrence Logan, the author of the book, is my father."

"Really?"

He nodded. "My brothers and I grew up in a house with the 'Focus on Family.'"

She paused beneath a street light and tilted her head to look at him. "And the reason for that subtle note of irritation in your voice?"

"Subtle, but not subtle enough, huh?"

"Maybe I'm just perceptive."

He shrugged. "My dad and I just didn't see eye to eye on a lot of things while I was growing up. And it frustrated him that he was this expert on family relationships who couldn't figure out his own son."

"I imagine it frustrated both of you," she said gently.

"You are perceptive."

"Unfortunately, not perceptive enough to delve into the psyche of a twelve-year-old boy." She sighed. "Do you know what he told me when I asked him what was going on in his mind?"

He shook his head.

"He told me that he hated his father."

"And in that moment, he did," Scott told her. "But that doesn't mean he doesn't still love him."

She frowned so intensely at that, he couldn't help but smile.

"Is everything always black or white to you, Alicia?"

"Of course not," she denied. "I just like things to make sense."

"All of your lives have been turned upside down," he said gently. "It's going to be a while before anything makes sense again."

"You're right," she said. "In the meantime, what am I supposed to do to help Joey?"

"You really want my advice?"

"So far, you're making more sense than any of the books I've read."

"Give him an outlet," he said. "A healthy way to burn off his frustration."

"Like a dartboard or basketball hoop in his bedroom?" Her tone was skeptical.

Scott shrugged. "You never know what might work."

"I hardly think Joey's going to be placated by the kind of toys that you use to appease your Peter Pan syndrome."

"*Attention Deficit Disorder,*" he corrected her.

"What?"

"I was diagnosed with ADD when I was a kid," he said, surprising himself as much as he could tell he'd surprised her with the admission.

It wasn't something he talked about, and he wasn't sure why he'd mentioned it now. Maybe it was because Alicia was a nurse so she'd be familiar with the symptoms, or maybe it was because she was looking at him with such genuine interest in those dark eyes. Not pity or concern, but interest. Or maybe it was just that he found it so easy to talk to her about almost anything. Whatever the reason, he found himself telling her about his experience.

"I always had trouble focusing on tasks for any extended period of time, got bored easily. I'd take notes through the first half of a class, then tune out and start to think about something else. School was a real struggle, my grades always borderline.

"I don't know if I had a severe enough case to warrant medication, but I know my father didn't think so. Or maybe he was just afraid that if I actually had a prescription, there would be a paper trail that some enterprising young journalist might use to prove that Dr. Lawrence Logan wasn't as all-powerful and all-knowing as he wanted the world to believe. He actually had a kid who was a screwup.

"But maybe he was right, because over the years, I've learned to control it. Sometimes on a case I'll be stuck in my car for extended periods of time, so I've had to control it. But when I'm in the office for too long, I start to get antsy and I find that tossing a few darts or shooting some baskets helps."

"ADD isn't anything to be ashamed of," she told him.

"I'm not," he said. "Or maybe I am. It's not something I usually tell people about. And in a family of overachievers, I was something of an oddity.

"Until I went into the police academy, I had no clear goals, no concrete ambitions. And then—" he shrugged "—as it turned out, I couldn't stick it out there, either."

"What happened with Freddie—that's the kind of blow that would have shaken anyone."

He shrugged again, pretending it didn't matter, but the truth was that her understanding meant a lot. Maybe too much.

"The point is, I might understand Joey better than you realize. Not that I'm suggesting he has ADD or ADHD or whatever else they're calling it these days, just that I know what it's like to feel as if you have no control over your own life—and the anger and frustration that invariably go along with that."

"Sounds like you have more of a handle on his feelings than I do."

"You were never a twelve-year-old boy," he pointed out.

"You've got me there." She sighed. "I have to admit, there are days when I miss the little boy with wonder in his eyes and a shy smile on his face."

She shook her head, as if shaking off the melancholy. "Sorry—we're almost back at the house and I haven't given you a chance to talk about whatever it was you wanted to discuss."

"Joe's ex-wife."

"You want to know about Yvette Solomon?" Alicia asked the question with obvious reluctance. "Why?"

"Because I'm trying to get a complete picture of Joe's family, and she's a missing piece."

"They've been divorced more than five years now, and as I said, she hardly has any contact with either him or the kids."

"Joey told me that his mother claimed Lia wasn't Joe's child."

"My usually closemouthed nephew didn't hold anything back, did he?" She shook her head. "I didn't even realize he knew what Yvette said about Lia. I'm sure Lia doesn't know—she would be devastated by the thought that Joe might not be her daddy."

He frowned. "You mean your brother didn't insist on a paternity test?"

She shook her head. "Yvette dropped her little bomb in the middle of the custody battle, even going so far as to ask the judge to change Lia's last name to Solomon, her maiden name. The judge was going to order a test and have the hearing adjourned until the results came in, but Joe asked him not to. He said he didn't need a lab report to know that Lia was his daughter. Regardless of the blood flowing through her veins, she was his.

"He loves those kids more than anything," Alicia continued softly. "Which is why it's so hard for me to understand why he would let himself be sent to jail."

"In all fairness to your brother," he said dryly, "I don't think going to jail was his choice."

"I know," she said. "But I can't help feeling there was something he could have said or done that would have made a difference. Even an explanation about why he didn't testify might make a difference to Joey and Lia."

"I think having you here is making a difference," he said.

"I don't know if that's true, but I do know there isn't anywhere else I could be." She glanced at her watch. "And right now, I need to check on Ail Zerauj—because her light is still on and it's past her bedtime."

And in that moment, the light went on for him. "It's backwards."

Alicia frowned. "Yes, she told us about it at dinner."

"Not Lia's name," he said. "Nomolos—the name on the cell phone registration. 'Nomolos' is 'Solomon' spelled backwards."

Chapter Seven

Scott was beginning to despair of finding evidence to exonerate Joe Juarez.

He'd reviewed Jordan's client file. Of course, there wasn't much in it so that didn't take long. From what he knew of the case, it had been dumped on Jordan's desk at the eleventh hour and the trial judge had refused to give him a postponement to conduct any kind of independent investigation or plan a defense.

He'd also read the trial transcripts, and he couldn't believe some of the outrageous rulings made by the Honorable Judge Karl Rhinehardt. The judge had even sent Jordan to jail on contempt charges when he blew a gasket—justifiably, in Scott's opinion—in the courtroom.

An examination of the evidence showed it to be circumstantial at best and often contradictory. But the prosecution had called witness after witness to the stand, some of them testifying to nothing more than the fact that Joe worked for Russo's racing team.

The only one who clearly pointed a finger at Joe was Matt Lawrence, the son of one of his bosses. And if Jordan's notes were to be believed, apparently Matt had an axe to grind with Joe because of an altercation that took place at a local bar over some girl. Unfortunately, that wasn't even a theory he'd been able to use to challenge Matt's testimony because no one knew the name of the girl.

Scott suspected that the A.D.A. had known how flimsy her case was and just threw everything she could at the jury, hoping that something would stick. Unfortunately for Joe Juarez, something did.

And so far, Scott hadn't found anything solid to support an alternative theory of the case.

He'd managed to track down Yvette Solomon at one of the seedier motels in a rougher part of town. Joe's ex-wife had been belligerent, uncooperative and downright rude. But beneath the surface, he'd sensed nerves and fear.

He'd decided the woman was definitely hiding something despite her claims that she hadn't seen Joe in months, didn't own a cell phone, and if Scott didn't get out of her room before her boyfriend got back, he was going to regret it. He had yet to confirm the existence of the boyfriend Yvette had refused to name, but he'd made a note to follow up on that.

Frustrated that he had nothing else, Scott decided to take a break, tossed a few darts at the board on the wall across from his desk, then spent the afternoon finishing up some paperwork on another case. Not in the mood to go home to an empty apartment and even emptier refrigerator, he ordered in some dinner and kept working. Or trying to work while thoughts of Alicia kept popping into his mind.

Maybe it was because he'd agreed to keep an eye on her and the kids that he felt compelled to do so. Or maybe his promise to Joe only gave him the excuse to do what he wanted to anyway. In either case, when he left the office Saturday night, he found himself heading to the Juarez home rather than to his own.

And he found Alicia sitting on the front step looking as sad and broken as the plastic pieces that were scattered across the grass.

Alicia wasn't entirely sure what she was waiting for.

She was old enough to know that no white knight was going to come riding to the rescue and set everything right in her world. And yet, what was the first thing she'd done when she'd stepped outside and saw the broken lawn ornaments? She'd called Scott.

She'd left a message on his machine at home, then she'd tried his cell phone and very nearly left a message there, too, before she remembered that it was Saturday and if he wasn't at home, it was probably because he was out on a date and the last thing he wanted was to have his evening interrupted by a client he was doing some cut-rate P.I. work for. So she'd hung up the phone, already regretting the impulse to call.

Or maybe it had been weakness more than impulse. She hated feeling weak, out of control. But so much of her life was out of her control these days. Her brother was in jail, his children were suffering, the future of her job was uncertain, and now this.

She tightened the arms that were wrapped around her knees, as if that might stop the trembling that shook her so deep inside.

She didn't understand why this had happened—couldn't comprehend how someone could be so maliciously destructive. But she knew the why and how didn't really matter. What mattered was the damage that had been done.

Her gaze was drawn reluctantly to the evidence strewn across the front lawn, and though her eyes were dry, her heart was weeping for the little girl sleeping inside.

Yeah, it was only a bunch of stupid lawn ornaments. But while the rational part of her brain recognized that truth, her heart couldn't get past the fact that they'd been Lia's stupid lawn ornaments. And she knew her niece would be devastated by the senseless vandalism. Even more so if she had to see the broken pieces that were all that remained of her plastic friends.

Alicia wanted to at least spare her that. And maybe, if she started to clean up the mess that was strewn across the lawn, she might start to feel a little better.

She heard the deep rumble of a car engine and glanced up to see Scott's vintage Corvette pull into the driveway. When he stepped out of the car, she realized she was trembling again.

"Alicia?"

She heard the concern in his voice, felt it in the hands that took hold of hers as he drew her to her feet.

She tried to respond, but her throat was suddenly tight. And when she tipped her head back to look at him, her eyes were suddenly blurred with tears.

He didn't say anything else. He simply pulled her

closer until she was cradled against his chest, and then he wrapped his arms around her.

The dam that had been holding the grief inside her broke wide open and the tears poured out.

She didn't know how long she'd been crying when he must have decided he wasn't going to stand forever in the middle of her brother's front porch and suddenly scooped her into his arms. Her breath caught as he lifted her feet off the ground and started into the house, then expelled again on a sob.

It occurred to her that maybe she should protest, but words were impossible. And trying to wiggle away from the tightly muscled man who held her so firmly would have been an exercise in futility. So she just buried her face against his chest and held on.

"I'm not running away with you." He murmured the words softly, his deep voice as comforting and reassuring as the arms enfolding her. "I just figured, if this was going to take a while, we should be comfortable."

He carried her through the front door, into the living room, and then settled down into the oversized chair she'd fallen asleep in the other night. He held her in his lap as a parent might hold a child. And she clung to him as if she were a child, and cried as if her tears would never run dry.

Finally, the storm of emotion passed, leaving her empty and achy.

"Feel better now?" he asked gently.

She nodded, her head still against his chest.

"Want to talk about it?"

This time she shook her head.

His hand stroked down her back, and up again. "I

noticed the lawn ornaments are gone," he said. "And I'm guessing the plastic pieces in the grass are what's left of them."

She nodded again.

"What I can't figure out is why this petty vandalism caused a complete meltdown in the woman who was more furious than upset when four perfectly good and reasonably expensive tires were slashed on her car."

Looking at it from that perspective, she could see why he'd be confused.

"They were Lia's lawn ornaments," she said and drew in a shaky breath as she fought back a new wave of tears.

His hand continued rubbing her back in a rhythmic motion that somehow managed to soothe and stir her at the same time. She was too much of an emotional wreck right now to deal with the unwanted feelings he evoked, so she concentrated on the soothing—and the strong, steady beat of his heart beneath her cheek.

"Okay," he said after a few more minutes had passed. "Let's get the story told and the tears all done, then we'll get the yard cleared up."

Alicia nodded and climbed out of his lap, and though Scott immediately missed the warmth of her in his arms, he could appreciate the wisdom of her retreat.

Because sometime in the midst of all the tears, he'd become conscious of the light, floral scent she was wearing, the fullness of the breasts pressed against his chest and the curve of her buttocks nestled against his groin. And he'd had to concentrate on the hands of the clock on the other side of the room to prevent all the blood from descending into his lap.

"I'll make coffee," she said now, already moving toward the kitchen.

"Don't you have anything stronger?"

"There's probably a beer in the fridge, if you'd prefer."

He had to smile. "I meant for you."

"Oh. Well." She'd already filled the tank with water and was measuring grounds into the filter. "I don't need anything stronger. I'm okay now. Really."

He nosed through the upper cupboards anyway until he discovered a bottle of Jameson's tucked away. While she turned the coffee on, he uncapped the bottle and poured a couple of fingers into a tumbler.

"It will help settle your nerves."

"I really don't drink anything stronger than wine," she told him, eyeing the amber liquid warily.

He pressed the glass into her hands. "Drink."

She lifted the glass to her mouth, took a tiny sip that barely moistened her lips. And still coughed and sputtered. "What is that—gasoline?"

"It's good Irish whiskey, and you need to drink more than that if it's going to do you any good."

She took another cautious sip, and though her eyes watered, she seemed to handle it. "I think the first swallow numbed my throat."

"That's the idea," he told her.

She sipped again. "Is it going to make me feel tingly like the wine?"

"Probably." He poured himself a cup of the coffee that had just finished brewing while she sipped again.

"I like that tingly feeling," she said, then looked away as her cheeks flushed with color.

He shook his head, amazed that a woman who looked

like a goddess of seduction could blush like a little girl. And intrigued to find out if he would discover passion or innocence when he took her to bed. Because with every day that passed, he became more certain that the attraction between them wouldn't be denied forever.

"I feel the same tingle when you look at me sometimes," she admitted. "Not when we're just talking about Joe's case or something like that, but when you really look at me, as if you're thinking of kissing me."

And revelations like that were making it increasingly difficult for him not to toss her over his shoulder, carry her to the nearest horizontal surface and find out.

She sent him a quick glance beneath lowered lashes as she sipped again. "Have you thought about kissing me?" she asked. "Or was I imagining that part?"

"No, you weren't imagining it." He took the now almost-empty glass away from her.

She pouted, drawing his attention to the luscious mouth that he'd spent far too much time fantasizing about.

"You told me to drink that," she reminded him.

"That was before I realized it was a little too heavy for a lightweight like you."

"But I was starting to like it."

He poured her a cup of coffee. "You were going to tell me about Lia's lawn ornaments."

"Oh, yeah." She sighed and sipped her coffee. "It all started because she wanted a kitten. She was four years old, I think, and begging Joe for one."

Scott pulled out a chair for her, then seated himself across from her.

"And Joe, well…" She paused to smile, but he noticed it was just a little sad. "Joe never could refuse her anything. Although he did let her wait a few months, to make sure she was serious about it. And on her fifth birthday, he took her down to the pound to pick out a kitten.

"Lia was absolutely ecstatic. But less than forty-eight hours later, Joey was in the hospital struggling to breathe."

"He was allergic to the kitten," he guessed.

She nodded. "And though she knew there wasn't any other choice, it broke Lia's heart to give up that kitten. She cried almost nonstop for a week, which broke her daddy's heart.

"Then, one day when they were at a friend's house, Joe heard Lia giggling. It was the first time in weeks that he'd heard her sound so happy and carefree. When he went to see what she was laughing at, she pointed out a plastic flamingo planted in the neighbor's lawn wearing Ray Charles sunglasses, its legs spinning in the wind."

Her fingers were wrapped tightly around her mug, but he knew her attention was fixed on the memory.

"So Joe went across the street and paid twenty dollars for a used plastic lawn ornament that probably wasn't worth five bucks brand-new just because it made her happy.

"A few months later, they found the flute-playing pig at a garage sale. And a few months after that, it was the cow with the straw hat. And so on.

"She still has a picture of that kitten on her dresser, but she loved those silly plastic animals almost as much as she loved Snowball."

"Does Lia know what happened?" he asked gently.

Alicia shook her head. "Not yet. Thankfully she was already in bed when I went outside and saw what happened. I don't even know *when* it happened. I didn't hear anything." She frowned at that. "How is it possible that I didn't hear anything?"

"Maybe it happened while you were getting Lia's bath ready. The sound of the running water might have drowned out the noise."

"Doesn't that seem like pretty convenient timing?"

He had to admire the sharpness of her mind despite the effects of the alcohol.

"Maybe," he agreed. "What about Joey? Did he hear anything?"

She shook her head. "He was next door with Randy. He saw it first, when he came home. I guess I should be glad that he did. I would have hated for Lia to wake up to that mess."

She pushed to her feet abruptly, wavered slightly before she caught the edge of the table for balance. "And she still will if I don't get out there and clean it up."

He rose to his feet, pushed her gently back into the chair. "I'll take care of it."

"You don't have to do that," she said. "This house and the kids are my responsibility."

"Alicia…" He shook his head. "Why is it so incredibly difficult for you to accept help when it's offered?"

"It's not. I mean, I appreciate the offer, but I can take care of it. Really. I'm not going to fall apart again.

"It probably wasn't even the broken decorations," she went on. "They were just the proverbial last straw. You know—the one that broke the mammal's back."

The sharpness of her mind, he mused, seemed to be in a state of flux.

"Yes, I know about that one," he assured her solemnly.

"And anyway, I've been bolstered up with Irish courage."

"You mean Dutch courage?"

She frowned. "You said it was Irish whiskey."

"You're right, it was." His lips twitched, but she seemed not to notice. "My mistake."

"So you see, I am okay, and I apologize for overreacting. I should never have called you to dump this problem in your lap. I should have handled it on my own."

She'd called him?

Now it was his turn to frown over that revelation.

"I need to stand on my two feet," she went on. "What kind of example am I setting for the kids if I run to someone else for help every time something goes wrong?"

"Don't Joey and Lia come to you when something goes wrong in their lives?" he countered.

"I hope so."

"Then why is it wrong for you to lean on someone else?"

"It's not, I guess." But she didn't sound entirely convinced. Then she asked, with more than a hint of challenge in her voice, "Who do you lean on?"

"My brothers."

"Really?"

He nodded. "We don't always see eye to eye on things. In fact, we rarely see eye to eye. But when the weight of the world gets too much for any one of us to handle, the others are always there."

"I can't imagine the weight of the world ever getting to be too much for you," she said.

"Well, it does. And it has."

"Like when Freddie died?" she probed gently.

It wasn't the first time she'd mentioned his name, but he stiffened automatically, as he still did whenever he thought about his former partner and close friend. But over time, the ache of the loss was gradually receding, the sharpness of the pain slowly fading. And though he was tempted, more out of habit than reluctance, to ignore her question, he figured she was entitled to know some of his secrets in exchange for her willingness to share her own.

"Yeah," he admitted. "Like when Freddie died. I'm not sure I would have got through that time without LJ and Ryan and Jake, especially after—"

No, he stopped there. No point in spilling all of his dark secrets.

But Alicia picked up the thread without hesitation. "After your girlfriend walked out?"

"You and Aster must have had quite the conversation," he muttered.

She smiled easily, unapologetically. "She wanted to make sure I had the scoop on my hunky P.I."

He cleared his throat. "You shouldn't believe everything Aster tells you."

"Then your girlfriend didn't run out?"

"Well, that part is true," he admitted.

And though it wasn't an event that had brought the weight of the world down on him, it wasn't something he particularly wanted to discuss, either.

But Alicia, thankfully, didn't push the issue. All she said was, "I'm glad your brothers were there for you."

And in the softly spoken comment, he heard just as clearly what she didn't say—that her brother wasn't there for her. Not anymore.

"I'll go clean up the lawn," he said.

This time she didn't protest, but only said, "Thank you."

"I wish you'd stop thanking me," he said, uncomfortable with her gratitude. Because the very last thing he wanted was for Alicia to feel as if she owed him anything.

"Are you going to bill me for this hour?"

He turned in the foyer to scowl at her, offended that such a thought would even cross her mind. "Of course not."

She smiled smugly, as if his response was no less than she'd expected. "Then you'll just have to accept my gratitude."

And then, still smiling, she took a step closer.

He would have taken a step back, but there was nowhere to go. She was in front of him, the wall was at his back, and his access to the door was blocked by her body, his escape route effectively barred.

And he felt suddenly and desperately in need of an escape route. Because although she was looking at him with that enchanting sparkle in her dark eyes and those luscious lips were temptingly curved, he needed to remember that Alicia Juarez was a woman who wanted a ring on her finger and babies in her future. She certainly wasn't the type of woman who engaged in casual affairs, and he couldn't offer her any more than that. Although the realization left him feeling strangely defeated, it also renewed his determination to do the right thing.

"Good night, Alicia."

"Good night," she said.

But she didn't move away so he could reach the door. Instead, she rose up on her toes and pressed her lips to his.

It was the softest touch, the briefest taste, and it stirred in him a powerful hunger for more. So much more.

He stood his ground, held his hands at his sides, even though what he really wanted was to haul her into his arms again and devour that sweet lush mouth. Instead he waited, endlessly, achingly, for the kiss to end.

But her lips continued to move over his, softly, sweetly, irresistibly. Her eyes drifted shut and her body swayed closer. And, well, the strength of his resistance wasn't nearly as powerful as his hunger for her.

His arms wrapped around her, pulled her against his body. She pressed even closer, so that her breasts were crushed against his chest and all of the blood rushed out of his head. His hands slid up her back and down again, over the curve of her buttocks. She murmured her appreciation and continued to kiss him in that unhurried, patient way that was quickly driving him to the brink.

Then the tip of her tongue flicked tentatively over his lips, and he felt himself teetering on the edge of reason. For sanity's sake, hers as well as his own, he pulled back—so fast he rapped his head against the wall.

He swore, Alicia blinked, and the fog of desire that had enfolded both of them in its embrace suddenly dissipated like the morning mist.

Chapter Eight

Nancy Logan stared at the skeins of baby-soft yarn in her hand and fought against the tears that burned the back of her throat. She already had the pattern and the needles in her basket, but she couldn't decide between the butter yellow and the mint green.

Not a life-altering decision by any stretch of the imagination and not one that would have her on the verge of tears on an ordinary day. Then again, she hadn't had many "ordinary" days in the last few months—and none at all since Robbie had gone.

She had his letter in her purse, had been carrying it everywhere with her since it had arrived in the mail three days earlier. A letter she'd read so many times now that she had the words memorized, but she still pulled it out of the envelope every chance she got, just to look at the writing. Sometimes she'd trace a finger over the bold script, as if touching the paper he had touched would convince her he wasn't so very far away.

And maybe he wasn't. She really didn't know because she had no idea where he'd gone. The letter had been postmarked Las Vegas, but she knew that only proved he'd been there when he'd dropped it into the mail.

Maybe he was still there. Maybe he was halfway to the East coast. Or maybe he was finally heading home.

No, as much as her heart ached to believe that he would find his way back to her, she knew he was still moving in the other direction.

I'm sorry, Nancy. But I had to leave. I don't see that there was any other choice. Everything that's happened is because of me.

She could see the words on the page, hear his voice speaking them inside her head.

She wished he'd talked to her instead of sending a damn letter, then she could have told him that he was right—that everything good that had ever happened in her life had happened because of him.

But Robbie had dealt with this latest crisis at the Children's Connection in the only way he knew how— by leaving.

Oh, Robbie, she thought, her eyes blurring with tears. How much of your life are going to spend running away from those who care about you? How could you not know how much I love you? How much I need you?

She felt the wave of emotion flow through her. Frustration and anger. Sadness and grief. And the hurt— slashing and deep—that the man she loved so much and who claimed to love her could walk away from the life they'd started to build together. And the tiny life growing inside her.

She didn't care that he hadn't known she was pregnant when he left, and though she didn't want to use their baby to make him come home, she wasn't going to let their child grow up without a father. She wasn't going to let him do to this baby what Jolene and Lester had done to him. She wasn't going to let their child believe he didn't matter.

Or *she,* she amended quickly, acknowledging that the tiny life she carried might be a girl.

Boy or girl, she knew she would love this baby as much as she loved the baby's father. And hurt and anger aside, she did love Robbie—even if she wanted to kick his ass all the way from here to Vegas for running out on her the way he'd done.

She put both colors of yarn back on the shelf along with the pattern and needles.

She wasn't going to spend the next five months sitting at home knitting baby blankets. There would be plenty of time for that after she found her husband.

What Alicia found when she woke up Sunday morning was that too much whiskey could leave a bad taste in the mouth, a sharp pain in the skull, and—as the memories of her reckless behavior the night before flooded her brain—a load of humiliation heaped upon her shoulders.

She pushed aside the covers and squinted at the clock beside her bed. It was just a little past seven and quiet enough that she could be certain Joey and Lia were still asleep. She was tempted to grab a few more minutes under the covers herself, but she swung her feet to the floor and made her way to the bathroom where she swallowed a handful of aspirin with water from the tap, then brushed her teeth and rinsed with mouthwash.

She pulled on some clothes, then headed to the kitchen. The kids might be sleeping now, but they would be up soon and then she was going to have to tell Lia what had happened the night before. But as she whisked together eggs and milk to make French toast, it wasn't the lawn ornaments on her mind but the kiss.

She'd initiated the contact. She could acknowledge and accept that fact. She'd wanted to kiss him—another undeniable fact. And the alcohol had loosened her inhibitions enough to allow her to act on that want.

But she'd underestimated him—or maybe it was her own reaction that she'd been unprepared for. She couldn't remember ever wanting like this before—so strongly and fiercely.

With Ross, it had been more of a slow, steadily building attraction. With Scott, it was as if she'd been buried by an avalanche of need the moment their lips had touched. Even now, she could feel the firm slide of his mouth over hers, the leisurely stroke of his hands on her skin, the bold press of his body against hers.

She closed her eyes and let out a long, shaky breath.

What made the situation even more complicated was that she liked him. If it was just a physical attraction, she could deal with that. Maybe even indulge in the simple pleasure of being with him.

But the more she got to know Scott Logan, the more she realized that he wasn't a simple man. He was serious and intense, a man who lived his life according to the tenets of right and decency and honor. The kind of man she could all too easily lose her heart to. And she had no intention of losing her heart. Not ever again.

With that thought in mind, she decided to take her coffee out to the porch while she waited for the kids to wake up. The colorful broken plastic pieces that had been scattered in the yard the night before were nothing more than a memory now. Scott had obviously done a thorough job—

The thought froze in her mind as she stared at the faded pink flamingo with sunglasses, the banjo-strumming frog, the overall-wearing cow, the flamingo with the top hat facing the one wearing a lei, and the flute-playing pig.

She moved in for a closer inspection, noted that the handle on the banjo was broken and the cow was missing part of one leg. But the other minor chips and defects were almost as invisible as the glue holding the cracked pieces together.

She moved back to the step, her forgotten cup of coffee still clutched in her hands, and sank down.

He'd fixed Lia's animals.

She couldn't believe it—wouldn't have believed it was even possible. But he'd done it.

And the heart that she'd so recently vowed to protect pretty much just went *splat*.

Scott was having trouble focusing on his work. Or maybe he was just having trouble focusing. He scrubbed a hand over his face as he yawned. He should probably go back home to bed, where he'd spent precious little time after finally piecing and gluing Lia's lawn ornaments back together.

Maybe he shouldn't have bothered—it wasn't as if she wouldn't be able to tell they'd been broken. But it had occurred to him, as he'd been picking up the pieces, that some of the characters might be fixable. And once that thought was in his mind, he'd been compelled to find out. To salvage what he could for the little girl who had already lost so much.

When he was finished, he hadn't thought they'd looked too bad—except that the legs on the flamingo with the sunglasses wobbled like crazy when they turned. But at least they'd turned again. Not too bad for a guy who'd never had the attention span to finish a traditional jigsaw puzzle.

So he'd driven back to the Juarez house to stick the animals into the flower bed. By the time he was home again, the first hints of morning were starting to lighten the sky. Then he'd fallen into bed, wanting only a few hours of mindless slumber.

Instead, he'd dreamed.

He shook his head, pushed the memories of those dreams out of his mind.

"Scott?"

His head came up, and he wondered if the woman standing in his doorway was really there or if he was dreaming again.

"Uh, hi."

"Am I interrupting?" Alicia asked.

She'd been interrupting his life from the moment she walked into it, but he shook his head. "No, I was just trying to catch up on some things. Nothing important."

She took a tentative step into his office. "You fixed the lawn ornaments."

He couldn't help but smile at the wonder in her tone. "Yeah, it surprised me, too."

"I don't know how to thank you."

"Was Lia okay with them?"

She nodded. "She wanted to thank you herself, but I needed to come alone, to talk to you about something else, if you have a few minutes."

"Sure," he agreed, after a quick glance at his watch. "In fact, I have about twenty of them before I'm supposed to meet my brothers for lunch."

She took another step into the room but didn't say anything else.

"What's on your mind?" he asked.

"I've been thinking about last night," she finally blurted out.

Yeah, he'd been thinking about that, too. And thinking of her, as he'd done all through the night.

Even in his sleep, he'd thought of her, dreamed of her. He'd smelled her—that subtle yet unforgettable fragrance she wore. He'd tasted her—the dark erotic flavor of passion in her kiss. And he'd felt her—the silkiness of her hair, the fullness of her breasts, the press of her naked body against his.

Oh yeah, he'd dreamed about her, and it was so real, he'd awakened reaching for her—only to find the bed empty and his body aching for the fulfillment he'd tasted in his dreams.

"And—" she took a deep breath, finally lifted her eyes to his face "—I came here to apologize."

He frowned. "What for?"

Her cheeks flushed. "For coming on to you. For putting you in such a difficult position."

He couldn't help thinking she could put him in any position she wanted so long as she was naked with him, but he knew better than to voice such an opinion when she was clearly struggling with the repercussions of a simple kiss.

"And I'm worried," she admitted, "that you'll withdraw from Joe's case because of my…inappropriate behavior."

"Alicia," he said patiently. "It was a kiss."

"I know, but—"

"And if anything personal happens between us—or doesn't happen—it won't sway me from the job you hired me to do."

"Oh." She seemed surprised—and obviously relieved—by this assurance, and offered him a quick smile. "Thank you. For being so understanding."

Scott puzzled over that for a moment. "The thing is, I'm not sure I understand at all why you feel the need to apologize for a kiss I thought we both thoroughly enjoyed."

The color in her cheeks deepened. "Because I don't do things like that. Ever."

"You did last night."

She shook her head. "There were extenuating circumstances. It was an emotional day. And on top of that, I drank that whiskey."

"You make it sound as if you spent the afternoon tossing back shots of Jameson's."

"I'm not much of a drinker."

"Yeah, I got that part," he told her.

"Then you should understand I wouldn't have done

what I did if I hadn't been drinking. And I'm grateful that you were able to, uh, tolerate my advances."

He wanted to laugh, except he could tell by the expression on her face that she was dead serious—and mortified. He crossed the room to where she was standing.

"I'm not usually so forward," she said, eyeing him warily. "And although I know the alcohol isn't an excuse—"

"Alicia."

She frowned at the interruption but stopped rambling so he could speak.

"Didn't it occur to you that what happened might have been the result of chemistry rather than alcohol?"

She shook her head again. "I would never..."

Her eyes widened and her protest died on her lips when he settled his hands on her shoulders and drew her toward him.

"Have you been drinking this morning?" he asked.

Her confusion gave way to indignation. "Of course not—"

That was all he needed to hear before he covered her mouth with his own.

He'd startled her—that was evident in the soft breath she expelled, the abrupt stiffening of her posture and the hands that came up to his chest, as if she intended to push him away.

But she didn't push him away. And as his mouth moved over hers, he felt some of the tension slowly seeping from her body and tasted the sweetness of her hesitant response that was like the bloom of a flower gradually opening to the warmth of the sun.

His hands slid into her hair, combing through the

silky tresses to tip her head back, taking her slowly but inexorably deeper. He'd always enjoyed kissing as a pleasant precursor to greater intimacies. But right now, he was content to just kiss her. In that moment, with Alicia, he felt as though he could gladly have gone on just kissing her forever.

He reminded himself that he was supposed to be proving a point—letting Alicia know that there was a hell of a lot more going on between them than she wanted to admit. As she was kissing him back now, he figured the point had been made.

It was probably time to ease away, for both of them to take a step back, to let her think about this new development before they decided where to go from here. Then she pressed her body against his, and he stopped thinking about how or why this was happening as all the blood rushed out of his head and straight to his loins.

Though she was feeling anything but steady on her feet, Alicia stepped back, out of Scott's arms.

She just needed a moment to catch her breath, to reevaluate, and try to figure out what the hell had just happened.

Talk about tingles—*wow.*

Her whole body was humming like a live wire, and she knew if he touched her again in the next two seconds, she'd explode in a shower of sparks.

So she took another careful step back, needing both distance and oxygen to her brain to put the situation into perspective.

"What—" She swept her tongue over her bottom lip to moisten it, and tasted him again. Tasted not just his flavor but his hunger, and everything inside her quivered. "What was that for?" she finally managed.

"To clear up any misunderstandings," he told her. "To make sure you realize that what happened last night had nothing to do with anything except you and me."

"Oh."

"Is that clear now?"

She nodded.

What was clear, in her opinion, was that she was entering dangerous territory. Territory she'd fenced off years before with barbed wire and warning signs posted around the perimeter. What wasn't so clear was how to put back the fences that had been torn down while she was being thoroughly kissed by this tempting man.

"Good," he said. "Now I'm going to kiss you again— this time just because I want another taste of you."

That was all the warning she got. And this time, he was holding nothing back.

His mouth was hard and hot and hungry on hers. She couldn't get her breath, couldn't find her balance. So she grabbed hold of him and hung on.

She'd forgotten how it felt to want like this, to be wanted like this. And, oh, to be kissed like this.

No, she realized, he wasn't kissing her. Kissing was far too tame a word to describe what he was doing to her. His lips and his tongue and his teeth were devouring her. As she was devouring him right back—feasting on his flavor, wanting only to gobble him up in quick, greedy bites.

And his hands. Oh, my, his hands were doing some devouring of their own. Streaking over her body, as hard and hot and hungry as his mouth, making her tremble and sigh and ache.

His lips skimmed across her cheek, down her throat, over her collarbone. His hands moved under her sweater, over her ribs, cupped her breasts. Her nipples strained against the lacy fabric of her bra, and when his thumbs brushed over them, she gasped, arched, shuddered.

There was so much heat inside of her now, pulsing through her veins, pooling at her center. Too much heat. Too much need.

She was familiar enough with lust to recognize it, and honest enough to acknowledge that was what she was feeling right now. It should be easy to give in to it—to give in to what they both obviously wanted in the moment without a thought to the future. But there was too much going on in her life right now to indulge in even a casual affair.

With that thought in mind, she finally managed to pull away. But it took another few moments before she could catch her breath and speak.

"Okay," she said at last. "I obviously underestimated the chemistry."

"You're still underestimating it if you think we can take a step back and pretend none of this ever happened."

"I'm not suggesting we pretend anything, but we do need to take a step back. I can't deal with this…attraction on top of everything else."

"On the other hand, having sex could simplify things." He grinned. "It would sure cut through some of the tension."

She shook her head. "I don't doubt that I could fall into bed with you and have a really good time, but—"

"Why don't we test that theory?" he interrupted to suggest. "Just to be sure."

She wanted to smile, but she knew that if she let herself be charmed by him, she'd be naked and flat on her back in no time. "Because I don't get involved easily or lightly," she told him. "And because I don't have the time or energy for the complication of a personal relationship right now."

"And if you had the time and energy?" he prompted.

"I don't know," she admitted.

But, oh, she almost wished she did so that she could find out.

Scott knew she'd given him an honest answer, if not the one he'd been hoping for. Just as he knew he had no right to push for anything more, not when he couldn't offer her what she was looking for. Alicia was a forever kind of woman, and he was a one-night-at-a-time kind of man.

But for some reason, she was the one woman he couldn't get out of his mind. And when he headed over to the pub to meet his brothers for lunch, he was still thinking about her.

He caught up with Ryan as he was walking through the door, and they found LJ and Jake already seated at their usual table in the back. And Scott realized he'd been looking forward to this since Ryan had called yesterday afternoon to set up the meeting.

Over the past few years, they'd each been so busy with their own lives there had been few opportunities to get together like this. Since Jake and LJ had moved back to Portland, that had changed, and Scott found himself enjoying the time he spent with his brothers. There were times when they frustrated and annoyed him, but he couldn't imagine his life without them.

And he knew they felt the same way—which was why they were together today, to talk about family and how they might help their father reconcile with the brother he'd been estranged from for so long.

"Finding Robbie's the key," LJ decided, referring to their cousin, who had taken off to parts unknown as a result of the latest scandals.

"Well, then, let's get right on it," Ryan said dryly.

Jake smiled as he shook his head at his brothers. "Although LJ's statement might sound simplistic, I think he has a point. And I'm willing to bet Scott has contacts who might be able to help us out."

The other three men turned their attention to the youngest brother.

"I have contacts," he agreed. "What I don't have is a starting point."

"Nevada," LJ said.

"Really?"

"Nancy got a letter from Robbie, postmarked Las Vegas," Jake told them.

"Which doesn't prove anything except that he mailed it from there," Scott told them.

"He could be halfway to Zaire by now," Ryan added.

Jake shrugged. "It's a place to start."

"I'll make some calls—" Scott tried, and failed, to stifle another yawn. "Tomorrow."

LJ nodded. "Thanks."

"Big case keep you out late last night?" Ryan asked.

"More likely a pretty young client," Jake said.

"Really?" LJ couldn't resist piping in.

"I was talking to Alicia at the clinic," Jake continued. "She told me you were doing some work for her."

"Alicia," Ryan said, considering. "Is she the one I said was even prettier than her name?"

"That's the one," Jake said.

Scott scowled. "Aren't you a happily married man?"

"Yes," Jake agreed. "That doesn't make me blind."

"The dark-haired nurse with the big eyes and bigger…smile," Ryan continued with a smile.

"I can't believe I'm related to you degenerates." Scott shook his head, then narrowed his eyes on Ryan. "And how do you know her?"

"We haven't even met," he admitted. "But I was at the clinic one day and she walked by— I swear, I almost needed a defibrillator to get my heart working again." He grinned at the memory. "Do you think you could introduce us?"

"Not in a million years," Scott told him.

"Come on. If all she is to you is a client…" He let the thought trail off.

Deliberately, Scott knew. Trying to get a reaction from him, to determine if his relationship with Alicia was more than strictly professional.

Scott didn't respond. Partly because he wasn't going to give his brother the satisfaction. And partly because he just didn't know.

Chapter Nine

Scott managed to stay away from Alicia for the next three days. Not really avoiding her, just giving her time to figure out where she wanted their relationship to go. Giving himself time to do the same thing.

Not that he'd actually figured anything out in those three days, and he'd made even less progress on his investigation of her brother except to rule out both Judy Greer and Margo Walsh and most of the other women on his list as suspects. He'd also made some calls and set the ball rolling in Las Vegas in the hopes, futile though he suspected they might be, of finding Robbie still in Nevada.

But he put the Juarez case, his missing cousin and everything else out of his mind for now because it was Thursday and he had a date.

He donned a suit and tie in honor of the occasion, and even stopped at the florist on the way.

This was a big night for Lia, and he knew she'd been looking forward to it with both excitement and trepidation. She loved to dance—had eagerly twirled around the living room to demonstrate her part for him. But he also knew it was her first performance in front of an audience, and she was sad her father wouldn't be there to see it.

"Daddy bought it for me," she told Scott when she showed him her costume. "And he said he couldn't wait to see me wear it on stage." Then her eyes had filled with tears, though she'd valiantly held them in check. "But he can't come because he's in jail now, so Aunt Alicia's going to take me. But there's another ticket if you wanted to come, too."

And there had been absolutely no way he could have refused.

A sentiment her brother obviously didn't share as Joey answered the door wearing an old pair of jeans with holes in both knees and a T-shirt with a picture of The Gruesomes on it.

"You're not coming with us," Scott guessed.

The boy grinned as he shook his head. "Saved by a social studies project. I get to spend the night next door with Randy, researching the aboriginal peoples of Australia instead of watching my sister twirl in a tutu."

"When's the project due?"

"Tomorrow."

Scott had given the same last-minute attention to his own homework when he was a kid, so all he said was, "Good luck."

"You, too," Joey said, picking up his backpack on the way to the door.

"Joey, did I hear…" Alicia's question trailed off when she came around the corner and saw him. "Oh, hi."

She was wearing a red dress that highlighted the dusky gold tone of her skin. The vee at the front dipped just low enough to reveal a hint of cleavage, and the skirt nipped in at her waist, then flared out to swirl around her knees. She'd put on makeup so that her eyes were somehow even bigger and darker than usual, and her lips glistened the same vibrant color as her dress.

He'd always been intrigued by her combination of sweet and sexy, but tonight the emphasis was definitely on *sexy*. It took Scott a full minute to catch his breath, another few seconds before he could untangle his tongue to speak.

"You look…amazing."

"Thank you," she said, her cheeks flushing with a color deeper than the one she'd brushed on. "You look nice, too. But…um…what are you doing here?"

Apparently Lia had neglected to inform her aunt of the invitation she'd issued. "Your niece and I have a date."

"Oh."

And then Lia came racing into the room. "You came."

"Well, of course I did. And—" he offered her the bouquet of tulips he'd been hiding behind his back "—these are for you."

Her eyes grew wide, her smile even wider. "Thank you," she whispered the words as carefully as she accepted the flowers, then she touched her lips to his cheek.

And he suddenly found himself in danger of losing his heart to this four-foot-nothing angel.

"Why don't you go find your shoes while I get a vase for your flowers?" Alicia suggested to the little girl.

Glancing up, Scott caught the glimmer of tears in her eyes before she turned away to reach into a cupboard.

"Did I do something wrong?" he asked after Lia had scampered away. He'd assumed flowers would be appropriate, but wondered now if he'd overstepped.

"No." Alicia filled the vase with water, then put the tulips in the water, fussing with them a little to rearrange the blooms. "You did something exactly right."

She set the vase in the center of the table and came over to kiss his cheek exactly as her niece had done. "Thank you."

And he realized he was in just as much danger of losing his heart here.

It was a magical night for her niece, and Alicia was glad for that. She knew Scott's presence hadn't made Lia forget Joe's absence, but he had helped make the event extra-special for her.

He'd even worn a suit and tie, affirming for Lia that it was a very important event. And making Alicia's mouth water at the realization that the man filled out a suit as nicely as he did a golf shirt and a pair of jeans. He'd also brought flowers—and the memory of the awe and wonder on her niece's face made Alicia misty-eyed all over again.

Or maybe it was watching the little girl on stage that was responsible for the tears that filled her eyes.

And Scott, somehow sensing the depth of her emotion even though his gaze was as intent on the stage as her own, took her hand in his and linked their fingers together.

After the performance, when Lia announced she was hungry, he'd suggested pizza. Then he'd picked up an extra large so they could take it back to share with Joey and Randy and Mrs. H.

She wondered about his willingness to hang out with not just her brother's children but the widow and her grandson who lived next door. And she worried that she couldn't appreciate the gracious gesture without suspecting he had ulterior motives. As if every kind and thoughtful act was part of his grand plan to get her into bed.

But if it was true, at least he was making an effort— which was a lot more than Ross had ever done. Her ex hadn't bothered to learn anything about her family or her friends or her interests. He'd just assumed if he bought her dinner he was entitled to some horizontal compensation.

Not that she'd objected. No, she'd been too blinded by the yearning in her own heart to realize that she was being used.

And she was wary of feeling that same yearning now.

No, it wasn't the same. It was stronger and deeper, and with every day that passed, it was getting harder and harder to ignore.

But she wasn't going to think about that now, she promised herself as they walked out of the pizzeria. Tonight was about celebrating Lia, and Alicia wasn't going to let her troubled thoughts or self-doubts or anything else ruin it.

Until they crossed paths with Jane French in the parking lot.

As Alicia stood back with her niece's hand gripped tightly in her own and watched the woman greet Scott, she felt everything inside her grow cold, colder. It wasn't the smile or the hug that bothered her, though she recognized the kind of casual affection that spoke of shared intimacy. It was the recognition that slapped her like an icy hand.

She felt the A.D.A.'s eyes on her, could sense the question in them while Scott made the introductions. Obviously she recognized Alicia, as well, although she couldn't seem to remember where they might have met.

Alicia experienced no similar confusion. This was a woman she would never forget—the woman who had put her brother in prison.

"I'm sorry," Scott said when they were back in the car and on their way to Mrs. Harbison's.

She tried to shrug off her lingering discomfort, to sound reasonable when she was feeling anything but. "You couldn't know we'd run into her."

"No," he agreed. "But I know it was awkward for you."

"She didn't even remember me," Alicia said, making the effort to keep her voice low so Lia wouldn't hear their conversation, though she was still irritated by the realization that the woman who'd ruined her brother's life didn't even remember doing so. "She completely undermined me at the trial, destroyed my credibility in front of the jury, and she didn't even remember."

"I read the trial transcript," he reminded her. "You gave the testimony you were supposed to give."

She wasn't in the mood to be placated. "You might have warned me when I hired you that the A.D.A. who prosecuted my brother was your ex-girlfriend."

"I didn't know it at the time," he said. "Not until I got the transcript with her name on it."

She stared straight ahead out the window. "You still should have told me that you had a conflict of interest."

"But I don't. My relationship with Jane ended long before you ever walked into my office, and her name on some court documents isn't going to stop me from doing my job."

But Alicia couldn't dismiss the other woman as easily from her mind as he had from the conversation.

Especially when she considered that the A.D.A. bore more than a surface resemblance to the woman Ross Harmon had married after letting Alicia know that she could never fit into his world. It wasn't just that they were both blue-eyed blondes, although they were. It was that they'd both clearly been born into a world where Alicia—even if she someday earned the M.D. she wanted to put behind her name—would never belong.

Ross's fiancée was a society girl with the money and connections that, in addition to his own, couldn't help but further his career. Although Ross had claimed to admire Alicia's dark beauty and fiery passion, the hard truth was that he'd enjoyed taking her to his bed but never intended their relationship to go any further than that.

Scott's ex-girlfriend might not be able to trace her ancestry back to the Mayflower, but she had the kind of cool sophistication and confident self-assurance that was indicative of wealth and privilege. And though Scott had let Alicia know he was attracted to her and wouldn't object to a physical relationship, he'd also made it clear that he wasn't looking for any more than that.

Well, at least he'd been honest about that from the get-go, which was more than she could say about Ross, who'd strung her along with promises and lies. And truthfully, she wasn't in a position to consider any kind of deeper involvement at the present time, anyway. Right now her brother and his kids were her priorities. Everything else—even her plans for med school and especially her suddenly overactive libido—was secondary.

Joe's heart broke every time he had to walk into the room with a guard at his back for his weekly visit with his children. They sat so still, so quiet and solemn and well-behaved. It was as if they'd suddenly turned into little adults with the weight of the world on their narrow shoulders.

It was his fault, he knew that. He was the one who'd destroyed their trust in him, undermined their faith, stolen their childlike innocence. And it broke his heart.

He'd been sentenced to spend the next five years of his life in a cell. He would gladly add another five to that sentence if he could somehow have spared them this. There was nothing he wanted so much as he wanted to hear his son laugh again, watch his daughter dance again.

He remembered, so clearly, the day Joey was born. He'd been in the delivery room with Yvette, and when they'd given him his son—when the nurse had placed the tiny, squalling bundle of red, wrinkled skin still protesting the indignation of his birth into his hands—his heart had completely melted.

With Lia, Yvette's labor was shorter, faster, harder. Not uncommon for a second birth, the doctor assured them. But his nonchalant demeanor was quickly eclipsed by the barking of frantic orders when Lia was finally pushed out into his hands—her body still, quiet, and the palest shade of blue. And Joe's heart had stopped until his daughter's was beating again.

It was hard to believe that had been eight years ago. The memories were so vivid despite the passage of time, despite how much they'd grown.

The next five years wouldn't move as quickly for him. Because in the short time he'd been in prison already, he'd learned that minutes were like hours, hours like days, and days like years. Time was empty and endless.

By the time he would be released, these children would be at different stages in their lives. Lia would be a teenager, thinking about boys instead of ballet, and Joey would probably be thinking about cars and college.

But for now they were still children. *His* children. And he was going to cherish every minute he had with them, even when they were spent in this cold, barren room.

Lia, always so shy and quiet when they came to visit, was a little more talkative today, wanting to tell him about her dance recital in great detail. But he noticed there was a lot of talk about Scott Logan, too. Apparently the P.I. had not only gone to Lia's recital with Alicia, but he'd given Lia flowers and bought everyone pizza afterward. And though Joe was thrilled that the evening had been a success for his daughter, he couldn't help but resent that Scott Logan had been there in his stead.

And where Lia left off extolling the other man's virtues, his son picked up. He talked about playing computer games and shooting hoops with him—the kind of things Joe used to do with his son. He had no right to be annoyed—not when he'd asked Logan to keep an eye on his family. He just hadn't expected he would be keeping such a close eye.

"Sounds like you've been seeing a lot of Scott Logan," he commented.

"He comes around all the time to see Aunt Alicia," Joey said.

"He does not," Alicia protested.

But her cheeks flushed, and Joe found himself noticing—possibly for the first time ever—how beautiful his sister was. He also noticed that she was at least halfway in love with Logan already.

He'd abandoned his family and stuck his sister with the responsibility of his children for the next five years. She'd always put everyone else's wants and needs before her own, and she deserved to be with someone who appreciated the incredibly loving and giving person she was. He should be happy that she'd found someone.

But he had sincere reservations about Scott Logan being that someone, especially when he remembered what Yvette had said.

When Jack's unhappy, people get hurt.

And he wished that it was anyone but Logan who had put that glow in her cheeks. Because the P.I. could ruin everything for all of them.

It was getting more and more difficult for Scott to justify his frequent visits to the Juarez home.

How many times could he claim to want to update Alicia on the progress of an investigation that had seen almost none? And though he hadn't taken on the case with any great expectations, even he was getting discouraged. He could only imagine how frustrating it must be for her.

Not that she ever complained or criticized him for not doing more or working faster. No—she would just nod, force a smile and say "Thanks." But he could see the worry that clouded those beautiful dark eyes and he would resolve to somehow do more and work faster—as if he wasn't already doing everything that could be done.

But he kept stopping by the house on Greenleaf Drive because he'd promised her brother that he would keep an eye on Alicia and the kids. At least, that was how he justified the visits in his own mind. Because he didn't want to admit the truth—that it was a lot more enjoyable to spend a couple of hours with Alicia and her nephew and niece than to pass that time alone in his empty apartment.

And he did enjoy being with all of them, which came as something of a surprise to a man who had so little experience with kids.

Then again, it wasn't as if they were babies who ran around in stinky diapers or toddlers who pelted him with building blocks. Joey and Lia were actually little people with thoughts and opinions and—in Joey's case—sometimes a lot of attitude.

But for the most part, they were really easy to be with. And it sure wasn't a hardship to shoot hoops in the driveway with the boy and his friend from next door, or to sit with the girl and listen to her read from a storybook, as she liked to do before she went off to bed.

Yeah, the kids were pretty easy.

It was Alicia who gave him the struggle.

After the sizzling kisses they'd shared in his office, he'd been optimistic that there would be more kissing and touching and other things in their future. But she'd shot down his hopes at every turn, clearly reestablishing the boundaries that had been breached and letting him know that sex was outside of those boundaries.

He'd accepted that she didn't want a personal relationship with him. Or he'd mostly accepted it, anyway. But the accepting didn't stop him from wanting, and every minute that he spent with her, he only wanted her more.

She had reasons for not getting involved, and he understood those reasons. He could even agree with most of them. But the understanding and agreeing didn't stop the wanting, either.

He knew he needed to distance himself from the situation and his growing feelings for her. Because he did have feelings for her, beyond the usual wanting to get a woman naked and horizontal. Although naked and vertical was sometimes good, too. Unfortunately, naked in any direction wasn't happening with Alicia, and he should have been looking to cut his losses and move on.

But he actually enjoyed being with her. Just sitting and talking—not just listening, but actually talking. Somehow he found himself talking to her more than he could remember talking to anyone else.

When he and Janie split up, he'd resigned himself to being alone. He just didn't have it in him anymore to get involved in anything that resembled a real relationship. Good times and great sex—sure. But anything beyond that—no way and no thank you.

Marriage and babies and all the other things most women wanted just weren't in the cards for him. He wasn't capable of giving his heart—wasn't sure there was anything left to give.

It was as if he'd just shut down emotionally after Freddie died. Everything that happened in that moment had been so sharp and dark and deep. Then the pain and grief and guilt had simply overwhelmed him. Janie had stuck it out with him for a while, he had to give her credit for that. She'd tried to be there for him, but he'd pushed her away. He'd had nothing to give her simply because there'd been nothing left.

From the beginning, Alicia had recognized that they had different expectations. And she'd been smart enough not to take him up on his good time offer. A woman as sweet and good as Alicia deserved a hell of a lot better than to hook up with a guy like him, even temporarily.

And if she hadn't already come to that decision on her own, he knew their chance encounter with Janie would have done it for her. Yeah, having been romantically involved with the woman who put her brother in jail wasn't a mark in his favor.

One step forward, two steps back.

But he still enjoyed the time he spent with Alicia. And since he figured it would last only so long as his investigation into the charges against her brother, he was going to continue to enjoy it.

She was wiping her hands on a dish towel when she responded to his knock on the door. "Is it just coincidence that whenever you stop by I seem to be taking dinner out of the oven?"

The warmth of her smile made him smile back.

In the last couple of years, he'd been so grimly focused on going through the motions of his life he hadn't found much reason to smile. It was easier with Alicia somehow. Everything was easier with her.

"I'd think of it as a lucky coincidence if you invited me to stay," he told her.

"Come on in. I just finished up a salad to go with the lasagna."

"Smells great," he said, reminding himself that it was not only inappropriate but rude to stare at the sweet curve of her butt as he followed her into the kitchen. But he snuck a couple of quick glances anyway.

"It's one of my mother's recipes—so I'll warn you in advance that it's a little spicy."

He frowned at that. "If the kids can handle it, I'm sure I can."

"Lia loves it," she told him. "Joey, not so much. That's why I usually only make it when he's not going to be home for dinner."

"Where is he?"

"Soccer camp."

"That's right." He remembered the kid telling him about it earlier in the week. "He's gone for the whole weekend, isn't he?"

"Yeah." She sprinkled grated cheese over a loaf of French bread and popped it under the broiler. "And Lia's spending the night with a friend, so it's doubly nice to have company. I forgot how quiet things are when they're not around."

Scott was suddenly aware of the quiet, too.

And suddenly, excruciatingly aware that Alicia was on her own not just for dinner but for the whole night.

"It's the first time Lia's spent a night away since Joe was arrested," she told him. "And though I was hesitant to agree, I think it's a good sign that she wanted to go."

Good for her, maybe. He wasn't so sure it was good for him.

The kids had always been a buffer against his growing desire for Alicia—their presence a constant reminder of all the reasons he shouldn't pursue his attraction to her. Any time he was tempted, he only had to gaze into Lia's soulful eyes or take in Joey's angry scowl and remember that Alicia had responsibilities he couldn't even begin to comprehend. Her brother's children came first for her—they had to.

But now, heaven help him, there were no adolescent chaperones anywhere in the vicinity. There was only Alicia—sweet and sexy Alicia—making his mouth water with a deep hunger that had nothing to do with the meal she'd prepared and everything to do with the woman.

"There's a bottle of wine on the counter, a corkscrew in the drawer. Why don't you open it while I'm dishing this up?"

Sweet and sexy Alicia.

A good bottle of valpolicella.

An empty house.

And hours and hours of the night still ahead.

No—he shook his head.

Very bad idea.

He should make an excuse—suddenly remember an appointment he forgot—and leave her to enjoy the peace and solitude alone. She would probably appreciate some quiet time, was just being polite when she'd invited him to stay.

But she was already cutting the lasagna, so he uncorked the bottle, poured the burgundy wine into two glasses.

He offered one to her, and when she reached for it, their hands touched.

She looked at him…and their eyes locked.

Time seemed to stop.

That single moment stretched out…wrapped around them…drew them closer.

Then was shattered by the earsplitting beep of the smoke alarm.

"The garlic bread," Alicia suddenly remembered.

He was left holding her glass while she turned to the oven, waves of thick smoke billowing out when she opened the door.

She coughed, waved ineffectually at the dark cloud with her oven mitt. Scott set down the wine to crank the handle of the window so the smoke would have somewhere to go.

The blaring of the alarm stopped as abruptly as it had started. Alicia finally pulled the pan of bread out of the oven, curls of smoke rising from the top of the blackened cheese.

She tapped the top gently with her finger, as if testing it for readiness. "I don't think it's done," she said. "I think it's dead."

And he couldn't help it—he laughed.

Then she laughed, too.

They stood there in the middle of a smoke-filled kitchen laughing like a couple of idiots over the demise of a loaf of garlic bread.

And she just looked so beautiful—with her eyes sparkling and cheeks glowing—he couldn't resist.

He kissed her.

Chapter Ten

Oh was Alicia's first thought, as his mouth came down on hers.

Then—*oh, my*—as his arms came around her.

And—*oh, yes*—as his tongue parted her lips to dip inside.

Then she didn't think at all, but closed her eyes and let herself be swept away by his kiss.

His arms tightened around her, pulling her closer to his hard body. His very hard, very aroused body.

She hummed with pleasure and appreciation, and she pressed herself against him. And heard the answering groan deep in his throat.

It was easy to remember all the reasons he was wrong for her, all the reasons they were wrong for each other—until he put his hands on her. Then reason didn't seem to matter. Nothing seemed to matter except that he was touching her.

As he was touching her now.

And then he released her as abruptly as he'd reached for her, took a step back and tucked his hands into his pockets.

"Alicia…"

She drew in a deep breath, tried to ignore the tingles that were dancing along her skin. Tingles of excitement, anticipation and hot, lusty desire.

She waited for him to say more—half expecting that he would make an excuse to go, and desperately hoping that he wouldn't.

There were a thousand reasons she shouldn't get any more involved with him. A thousand reasons she'd already discussed with him. And they'd agreed that it wouldn't be smart to indulge in any kind of deeper personal involvement.

But she wanted him.

She'd never known anything as huge and powerful and overwhelming as this need inside her. And though it scared her to need so much, what scared her even more was the emptiness she knew would be left inside if he walked away now.

But he didn't say anything else. He just continued to look at her in that way that made everything inside her feel hot and tight and tingly. And Alicia decided that, for once in her life, she wasn't going to worry about what was smart. She was going to stop being a coward and go after what she wanted.

"One of the great things about lasagna is that it's just as good when it's reheated," she said.

Okay, so it wasn't an explicit offer to go upstairs and have sex, but it was a big step for her. And Scott—she could tell by the flare of heat in eyes that she hadn't thought could burn any hotter—didn't seem to have any trouble interpreting her invitation. But he did seem to have trouble accepting it.

She could see the war waging between his desire to take what she was offering and—well, she really didn't know why he was hesitating. He'd made no secret of the fact that he was interested. But now, when she was ready to take that step, he was stepping back.

"You have no idea how tempted I am," he finally said.

"But," she prompted.

"But we want different things."

Yeah, that was one of those things they'd been clear about. He didn't see marriage and babies anywhere in his future, and she wanted a husband and a family in hers. But at the moment, she wasn't thinking any further into the future than the time it would take for them both to get naked.

"In the long term, that's true," she agreed. "Although I'm guessing that right now, we both want exactly the same thing."

"Screaming, sweaty sex?"

She knew he was being deliberately crude, thinking the harsh words would force her to reconsider. But the images evoked by those words only aroused her further.

"Screaming? Sweaty?" She smiled and took a step toward him. "God, I hope so."

He groaned. "Alicia—"

"You know, Scott, for a man of few words, you sure have a lot to say tonight." She lifted a hand, laid it on his chest, and felt the beat of his heart like a drum beneath her palm.

"I just want you to be very sure of what you're doing."

"It's the only thing I am sure of right now."

"And in the morning?"

She linked her arms around his neck and pulled his mouth down to hers. "We'll reevaluate then."

It seemed to take only that first touch of her lips to his for the last of his resolve to melt, then—*finally*—his hands were on her. He had such incredible hands. Strong and confident and somehow knowing all of the right places to touch.

She murmured her approval as they moved over her, hot and hard, seeking and stroking with delicious desperation. And everywhere he touched, she burned. Everywhere he touched, she yearned.

She yanked his shirt out of his jeans, eager to embark on her own exploration, anxious to feel the heat of his skin beneath her hands. His body was hard all over, so many glorious muscles under so much tantalizing skin. She wanted him naked—to touch him everywhere, taste him everywhere.

She tore her mouth from his. "Upstairs," she panted.

"What?" He looked as dazed as she felt, and she felt a surge of primal satisfaction that he was as crazy for her as she was for him.

"Upstairs," she repeated. "I don't want our first time to be on the kitchen table."

He scooped her into his arms, swinging her up so easily she lost her breath all over again. It was a foolishly romantic gesture, and one she'd never expected from him.

But as he started up the stairs, she realized that maybe

she should have. Because there were so many more facets to this man than she'd originally thought, so much still to uncover—if he would let her.

No—she wasn't going to go down that road. She refused to think of what might or might not be at another time. There was only now.

"Mine's the last room down the hall," she told him. "If you put me down, I can walk."

"Yeah, but I like the way you feel in my arms," he said.

And as her heart bumped inside her chest, she laid her cheek against his shoulder and let him carry her.

He put her back on her feet just outside of the bedroom and looked at her intently. "I just wanted to pause here for a minute to let you know that I'm going to try really hard to take my time with you, Alicia. But considering that I've been thinking about this for a couple of weeks now, I'm not making any promises."

"I'm not asking for any promises," she told him, and pushed open the door.

Then she found his mouth again, fused her lips to his and maneuvered him into the room, toward the bed. Somehow along that short path, she managed to tug his shirt over his head and unfasten the button on his jeans. Then, when she felt the backs of his legs bump against the mattress, she toppled him over onto it.

"So much for taking our time," he said, smiling against her lips.

She straddled his hips, let her hands stroke over the broad muscles of his chest, down the ripples of his abdomen. Then followed the same path with her mouth. She felt his heart pounding, tasted the salty tang of his skin, and reveled in the warm heat of this man. "Complaining?"

"Hell, no," he assured her. "Fast or slow is nego-tiable—I figure we'll manage some of both before the night is over." He groaned as her lips moved lower, as her tongue stroked over his skin. "But I have one rule that's unbreakable."

Curiosity had her lifting her head to ask, "What's that?"

He yanked her up so that she was lying flat on top of him, then rolled so that she was pinned beneath him on the mattress.

"Ladies first."

He quickly stripped away her clothes, then he used his hands and his mouth and his body with concentrated skill and single-minded effort to send her flying over the first peak.

And, oh, it was glorious.

As if she'd been shot through a rocket out of her own world and into the heavens where the air was liquid silver and the stars spun and swirled around her.

And when she finally floated back to earth, he was waiting there for her, waiting to send her up again.

And he did.

Then he rose above her, and finally, he filled her.

She arched beneath him, taking him deep inside, deeper. She found pleasure in the weight of his body on top of hers, the slide of his hard body against hers and the glorious friction of him inside her as they moved together in a timeless rhythm.

Then her body went taut, tightened around him, and with a deep groan of satisfaction, he flew into the abyss with her.

It was a long while later that they went back down to the kitchen for the dinner they'd abandoned earlier.

After the lasagna and salad had been eaten and the wine had been drunk, they cleaned up together. It had become a routine after dinner—he would wash, she would dry. Then they would share coffee and conversation.

Tonight, their routine was different. In between the washing and drying, there was a lot of kissing and touching, then more touching and kissing. And the hunger he thought had been sated reared up again.

He stripped away the silky robe she wore, anxious to put his hands on the silkier skin beneath. She quivered as he touched her, and the soft sexy sounds she made in her throat fueled the animal lust raging within him.

She offered no resistance or protest when he lowered her to the ground, but opened to him, embraced him, welcomed him. And he took her right there, on the cold tile floor with the lingering scent of burned cheese in the air. And he wondered afterward how it had seemed, for just a moment, like paradise.

"This is crazy," Scott said, after he'd managed to catch his breath and was able to speak again. "There's a perfectly good bed upstairs, and here we are, groping around on the kitchen floor."

"The groping part's over." Her lips curved. "Unless you're ready to go again?"

He chuckled and rolled off of her. "Give me a minute."

"You can take a few." She shifted so that she was sitting up, and whacked her elbow on a cupboard. "Ouch."

He sat up beside her, pulled her close, and was pleased when she tipped her head back against his shoulder. "Definitely the bed again next time."

She sighed heavily.

"What's on your mind?" he asked.

"I was just thinking about how happy I was, here with you, in this moment."

"Then why don't you sound happy?"

"Because I feel guilty about being happy when Joe's locked up behind bars," she admitted.

Though he was reluctant to let reality intrude, he knew that there were certain truths they both needed to face. "You know it's possible that I might not find anything to reopen your brother's case, don't you?"

She nodded.

"And if I don't, he's going to spend the next five years in prison."

She nodded again.

He stroked a hand down her arm, gently caressing. "Do you think he'd want you to be unhappy all of that time?"

"No. Of course not. I'm just being melancholic and stupid."

"No." He tipped her chin up. "Caring about your brother, wanting to make everything right for him, is just you being you. And it's only one of the things that makes you the incredible person you are."

Then he kissed her, leisurely, lingering, until he felt some of her tension seep away.

"Stupid, on the other hand," he said when he finally eased his lips from hers, "is the fact that we're both still sitting on this cold floor."

Alicia laughed, as he'd hoped she would.

Then she stood up and offered her hand to help him off the floor.

"I'm glad you decided to stop by for dinner tonight," she told him.

He grinned. "So am I."

And he lifted her into his arms and carried her back to bed.

A mistake, Alicia knew, often wasn't recognized as such until the damage was done.

And when she woke up the next morning in Scott's arms, she knew she'd made a very big mistake: she'd fallen in love.

She also knew that if she dared whisper those words to him, he'd be out of the door so fast he'd create a tailwind.

Of course, she'd known what his boundaries were from the beginning. She had no one but herself to blame for failing to respect those boundaries. She just wished, for once, that she'd had the good sense to fall in love with someone who might love her back. But no, she'd gone and tumbled head over heels for a man who'd told her from the outset he wasn't looking for a future with any woman.

Her heart, her problem.

And when it all came crashing down around her, she would deal with it.

She wasn't going to ruin it all now just because she knew that it would—eventually and inevitably—come crashing down. Instead, she would enjoy being with him for whatever time they might have, and she would lock the memories deep inside her heart where she could cherish them after he was gone.

She eased away from him and slid out of bed, determined to keep it casual, easy. No pressure, no expectations, no hint of what was in her heart.

But as she tightened the belt of her robe around her waist and headed down the stairs to make breakfast, she wondered how she could hide her feelings from him.

How could she pretend away something that was so huge, so all-encompassing, so unbelievably wonderful?

She didn't know how; she only knew that she had to do it. Because Scott didn't want her to love him any more than Ross had.

She'd made a lot of mistakes in her relationship with Ross, a lot of inaccurate assumptions. She'd been so blinded by love for him, she'd thought when he said, "I want you," he'd meant that he loved her, too. She'd thought when he told her he wouldn't ever get enough of her, it meant that he wanted to be with her forever.

She'd lived happily with this little fantasy for more than a year, until she'd learned through the usual hospital gossip that the perfectly wonderful Dr. Harmon had gotten engaged. Over poached salmon and champagne at the country club, one of the nurses whispered in revered tones. To his longtime girlfriend, someone else piped in, a pretty blue-eyed blonde whose parents had been friends with Ross's parents since their respective children were in diapers.

And Alicia had finally realized what a fool she'd been for ever thinking that a girl who grew up in a small apartment over her parents' roadside restaurant could have a future with a man who'd lived in a mansion with manicured lawns. But far worse, in her opinion, than Ross's deception was his suggestion that nothing should change between them because of his engagement. He wanted the perfect wife and the passionate mistress, and he honestly didn't seem to understand why she found that objectionable.

She'd been hurt and disillusioned, and every time she saw him at work, she was reminded of her humiliation.

In the end, she'd actually left her job at the hospital. That was when she'd taken a position at the Children's Connection and renewed her determination to focus on her own dreams of becoming a doctor and having a family of her own.

But now she was thirty years old and still had neither of those dreams in her sights.

She'd been wary of jumping into another relationship for the first while after her breakup with Ross. And she'd been busy with her new job, eagerly accepting every extra shift that was offered and working overtime every chance she got. She'd saved every penny that she didn't need for food and rent in a separate account for medical school.

Now her dreams had been put on hold again because she couldn't possibly afford the tuition or juggle the extra work of classes with caring for her brother's children, and it wouldn't be fair to them to even try. They might not be her own children, but they were family and they needed her. For Alicia, for now, that was enough.

Her night with Scott was just a temporary—and unexpectedly phenomenal—bonus.

And though she knew that Scott was nothing like Ross, she also knew that a future with Scott was equally unrealistic. She wouldn't regret the intimacy they'd shared. She couldn't regret something that had been so beautiful and perfect. But she also couldn't let herself weave fantasies around it. It was like a moment out of time—beautiful, surreal, and impossible to hold on to.

As she laid slices of bacon in the frying pan, she decided she wasn't going to dwell on that now. She wasn't going to worry about what might or might not be—she was just going to enjoy it, for however long it might last.

* * *

A mistake, in Scott's experience, was usually something that seemed like a good idea at the time but later came back to bite him in the ass.

Making love with Alicia had been a mistake.

Because even after he'd had her, he couldn't stop wanting her. After experiencing the pleasure of being with her, he only wanted her more.

He'd always believed that sex was a great tension reliever—the physical release an easy and pleasurable way to take the edge off. At least, that was how it had always worked before.

Maybe the problem was that he'd spent too much time thinking about Alicia, imagining what it would be like to touch her, dreaming about making love with her. Because what he'd found was that reality could actually sometimes surpass fantasy.

Now he was facing an unexpected dilemma: where to go from here?

Home—it was an immediate and instinctive response, and though he knew he was a louse for wanting to skip out on her after the night they'd spent together, he couldn't stay. He couldn't hang around and spend the day with her and do the things that couples did together because they weren't a couple.

It was just sex, he reminded himself as he threw off the sheets and got out of bed to gather his scattered clothing from the floor.

Screaming, sweaty sex—that was what they'd both wanted. And what they'd had in spectacular fashion.

Now the night was over. It was time to get dressed and move on.

He smelled fresh coffee and crisp bacon when he stepped into the kitchen. He saw only Alicia—looking soft and sweet and sexily rumpled. As he felt himself weakening, he cursed her for it.

"I have to go," he said abruptly.

Her smile didn't falter, but the light in her eyes dimmed just a little and he felt guilt prick at his conscience.

And wasn't this exactly why he'd decided, prior to showing up here last night, that he shouldn't get any more involved? Because Alicia wanted more than he could give, and she'd been as honest about that as he'd been about the fact he couldn't give it to her.

"Do you have time for breakfast first?"

"No, I'm, uh, late already. Thanks." Even he cringed as he said it—because the excuse not only sounded lame, it sounded as if he was thanking her for the sex.

But Alicia only cracked an egg into the frying pan and said, "Okay."

She didn't ask if he would come by later, and he didn't offer. The magic they'd discovered wrapped in one another's arms through the night didn't exist in the harsh light of day. It was a night he wouldn't forget—but also a night he knew wouldn't be repeated. They both had obligations and responsibilities they couldn't just pretend away—even if they wanted to.

So he left—he went back to his office, buried himself in work. But he couldn't stop thinking about her.

It was a fact that worried Scott as much as it annoyed him. He wasn't used to anyone getting under his skin, and Alicia had definitely got under his skin.

When he'd walked into the kitchen and found her cooking breakfast, he'd actually found himself thinking that he wouldn't mind starting every morning the same way—waking up with her, sharing breakfast with her, kissing her goodbye on his way out the door.

The vividness of the fantasy and the unexpected longing brought him up short. He hadn't thought about his future in a very long time, and he certainly hadn't thought about sharing his life with anyone. And it was a mistake, he knew, to let himself consider such thoughts now—especially about Alicia, whose visions of marriage and family were so diametrically opposed to his own.

He'd done the right thing by leaving. He had to nip it in the bud before Alicia got any ideas about marriage and babies and that kind of thing.

Yes, walking away was the smart thing to do.

Then again, no one had ever accused him of being smart.

Chapter Eleven

Scott saw a familiar gray head peek out the window next door when he pulled into Alicia's driveway Sunday night. Mrs. Harbison was like a one-woman Neighborhood Watch, up to date on all the comings and goings of the residents on Greenleaf Drive.

And, as he climbed out of his car, it occurred to him that he'd overlooked a potentially valuable source of information. Or maybe he was grasping at straws because he wanted to be able to tell Alicia he was making progress in the investigation when the truth was that he had a lot of suspicions but no proof of anything.

"Good evening, Mrs. H."

The neighbor responded to his greeting with a wave. "I thought that was your car I heard."

"You recognize the sound of my car?"

She grinned. "That kind of raw power in a sleek body—it can't help but catch your attention."

"Is that a polite way of complaining that my engine makes a lot of noise?"

"No one ever accused me of being polite," she told him. "If I was bothered by the noise, I'd let you know it."

He wasn't sure how to respond to that, so he said nothing.

"A sixty-six, is it?"

"You know your cars," he said, wondering if she'd learned about cars the same way Alicia had—from Joe.

But Mrs. H. shook her head. "Not really. Alicia told me the make and model— I just told her I like the way it looks."

He couldn't help but laugh at that. "Yeah, most women do."

"Is that why you have it?" she challenged. "To pick up women?"

"Just a fringe benefit," he assured her.

She smiled. "Well, I wasn't peeking my head out to be nosey, just to make sure I was right about it being you, make sure there was no trouble. This might not be a fancy neighborhood, but it's a good one and we all look out for one another."

"I guess there's not much that goes on around here that you don't know about," he commented.

"If you're wondering if I noticed that your car was parked in that very spot all through the night Friday night and well into Saturday morning, you bet I did."

And though there was humor rather than censure in her tone, he still felt like a little boy he'd been caught trampling flowers in the neighbor's garden. Which was probably a more appropriate analogy than he wanted to think about at the moment.

"Actually, that wasn't what I was wondering about," he said, although it confirmed his suspicion that this woman had her finger on the pulse of the neighborhood. "Do you think you could spare a few minutes to talk to me?"

"Time is something I've got a lot of these days," she told him. "Come on in. I have cookies to take out of the oven."

Alicia had been waiting for the knock.

She'd seen the headlights through the front window when Scott's car pulled into the driveway—almost an hour earlier.

Now, finally, he was at the door.

She hadn't seen or spoken to him since he'd turned down her offer of breakfast yesterday morning—after they'd spent the night together—and she was unexpectedly nervous now. She pressed a hand to the jittery nerves dancing in her belly as she walked to the door.

She reached for the handle, reminding herself to keep it easy and casual.

"Throwing me over for an older model?" she asked lightly.

"Have to consider it after sampling these amazing oatmeal chocolate chip cookies," he said.

Her gaze dropped to the plate in his hand. "Did you come by just to tease me with those, or are you going to share?"

"I might be persuaded to share, if you'll provide some coffee to go with them." He shuddered. "Mrs. H. offered me tea."

She smiled as she stepped away from the door. "I just made a fresh pot of coffee."

She filled two mugs and took them to the table.

Scott had taken the plastic wrap off of the plate, and Alicia passed his mug over so she'd have a free hand to take a cookie. He'd already bitten into one, she noted.

"What were you talking to Mrs. H. about?"

"Cars," he said.

"I know she likes yours." She nibbled on her cookie.

"That's what she told me. Almost makes the blood, sweat and tears worthwhile."

"You fixed it up yourself?"

"You sound surprised." He popped the last bite of his cookie into his mouth before taking another from the plate.

"I guess I never thought about it."

"I bought it a few months after Freddie died," he said. "When every part of my life was coming undone."

She sipped her coffee, wondering if he realized it was the first time he'd ever brought his friend's name into a conversation with her, wondering what it meant.

"My brother, Ryan, was with me," he continued. "I don't remember where we were going, just that he was with me when we drove past this old car parked on the side of the road with a For Sale sign in the window.

"Ryan thought it was a pile of junk, but he said, maybe you can make it into something, maybe you can't, but it would give you something to do instead of wallowing."

"Your brother sounds…interesting," she said.

He smiled. "He said something similar about you— wanted to know if I would introduce him to you."

"You talked to your brother about me?"

"All of my brothers were there," he admitted. "Actually, it was Jake who brought your name into the conversation."

"I'm not sure I want to know."

"All you need to know is that I turned down Ryan's request."

She raised her eyebrows.

"He would only try to steal you away from me," he explained.

"Do you think I'm that fickle?"

"No. I think you're too good for either one of us."

And though his tone was light, Alicia sensed that he really believed what he was saying, and she worried that he would pull away before they ever had a chance to see where things might go.

She got up from the table to refill her mug, and he followed.

"I'm not sure why I'm here, Alicia."

Easy and casual, she reminded herself again.

"You mean you didn't just come to deliver cookies?"

He shook his head. "I tried to stay away."

She'd expected as much, knew that for all of his talk about sex being just sex, he wasn't entirely comfortable with the intimacy they'd shared.

"I know you're not looking for a long-term relationship," she said.

"No," he admitted. "But—and this is as big a surprise to me as it is to you—I'm not looking for a meaningless one, either."

She smiled. "Well, that's something, then."

"But you deserve better than the little I can give you."

"Don't worry about me," she said. "I can look out for myself."

He pierced her with a look. "Can you?"

"Nothing happened between us that I didn't want to happen."

"It seems to me the wanting part is what's easy."

"Then why are you complicating it?"

He sighed even as he reached for her. "Hell if I know."

She went to him easily, eagerly, and cherished the feel of those strong arms around her.

"You're so sweet and warm and giving," he said.

She tipped her head back to look at him. "Why does that scare you?"

His smile was wry. "Because I'm not. I'm cold and selfish and cynical, and I worry that I'll rub off on you."

"Maybe I'll rub off on you." She smiled. "If we keep rubbing."

Scott laughed, amazed that she could lighten his dark moods so easily, even more amazed that he'd ever thought he could resist her.

"Is that an invitation?" he asked.

"Personally engraved."

And incredibly tempting. "But the kids—"

"—are sleeping." Her hands were already under his shirt, those eager talented fingers moving over his skin, nails scraping lightly. "So you can stay…for a while… if you want."

No doubt she could tell by the press of his erection against her belly how very much he wanted. And yet, he already felt guilty—torn between wanting to stay, hating to leave her before the night was over, and not wanting to want her as desperately as he did.

He *was* cold and selfish and cynical—at least, that was what Janie had said before she'd walked out the door.

And he couldn't dispute it. But now, with Alicia, he didn't feel cold but heat. And though he definitely wanted to take what she was offering, he also wanted to give.

"I want to stay…for a while."

She didn't say anything else, just took him by the hand and led him upstairs to her bedroom.

He closed the door and flipped the lock.

When he turned back to her, she was smiling at him in a way that made his breath lodge in his throat and his heart slam against his ribs.

Damn, she was beautiful. So unbelievably breathtakingly beautiful.

He quickly dispensed with the buttons down the front of her shirt, then parted the fabric to reveal pale dusky gold skin, lacy black bra. With lips and teeth and tongue, he nibbled his way down her throat, over the slope of her breast, felt her tremble.

And she was sexy. Irresistibly, mouthwateringly sexy.

He pushed the blouse over her shoulders, used the sleeves to imprison her arms behind her back. When his mouth closed over the peak of her nipple through the lacy fabric, she gasped and arched instinctively against him.

And seductive. So incredibly and enticingly seductive.

He dropped her blouse to the floor, her bra on top of it. Then he stripped away her skirt and panties to add them to the pile so that she stood in front of him, naked. Gloriously and stunningly naked.

Beautiful, sexy, seductive and naked.

And his.

At least for tonight, she belonged to him.

He wouldn't think about what had come before or what might come after, all that mattered was the here and now.

He carried her to the bed, laid her on top of the covers. "Scott…"

He didn't want to talk. He didn't have the words to express the wants and needs that were churning inside him. So he covered her mouth with his own, kissing her softly, slowly, deeply, as his hands stroked over the silky skin of her body. From her shoulders to her breasts and lower, skimming the dip of her waist, the flare of her hips.

He trailed his fingers over the smooth length of her thighs to her knees, then leisurely made his way back up again, stopping just short of the soft curls he knew he'd find at the apex. He felt her muscles tense and tremble, and her legs parted a little more, silently encouraging his continued exploration.

He retraced the same path, advancing just a little bit farther each time, then retreating again. Her breath hitched when he grazed the soft curls, then released when he retreated again. Another stroke, up and back down. Up again. She gasped when his thumb brushed over the nub at her center, her hips lifting instinctively.

His hands skimmed down her legs to wrap around her ankles, and he gently guided her feet into position, bending her knees, spreading her wide. Then he knelt between her thighs and lowered his head to taste her.

Her hips rose off the mattress again as his tongue slid between the moist folds of her womanhood. He slid his hands beneath her buttocks to hold her in position, to hold her captive against his mouth while he feasted on her.

She gasped and moaned, her hips rolling in unconscious rhythm as he tasted and took. When her body shuddered and tensed and finally went lax, he took more, driving her up again, pushing her beyond the limits of both of their endurance.

He couldn't give her much, but he could give her this. And in giving her pleasure, he found pleasure himself.

When she was cresting on the next wave, he quickly stripped away his own clothes. Then he rose up over her and plunged into her.

She wrapped herself around him, linked her arms around his neck, hooked her legs around his waist, anchoring him to her as they rode out the storm of sensation that battered them, together.

Scott didn't want to get Alicia's hopes up by telling her about his conversation with her brother's neighbor—at least not until he'd had an opportunity to confirm or refute what she'd told him. So he didn't say anything at all to her about it, but first thing the next morning, he made an appointment to see Joe's attorney.

"Thanks for squeezing me into your schedule," Scott said, seating himself across from Jordan Hall in the lawyer's office at Advocate Aid.

"I just got back from court, had some time. And, I have to admit, I'm a little curious about what progress you've made in your investigation."

"Unfortunately, not a lot."

Jordan smiled wryly. "Then I'll assume Joe's being as helpful as usual."

"Pretty much," he agreed. "But I did find out something interesting when I talked to Ethel Harbison yesterday."

"You say that as if the name should mean something to me," Jordan said.

"It doesn't?"

"Not ringing any bells," the lawyer told him.

"Joe's neighbor," Sarajane said, breezing into the office with two mugs of coffee and a smile. "Terrific lady—her grandson and Joe's son are good friends."

Scott nodded. "And I found out from Mrs. Harbison that, on the day the prototype and engine plans went missing, there was a car parked across the street. Mid-size, gray color, dark windows, spots of rust over the wheel wells. Maybe an old Accord, although she wasn't sure about that. But she was sure that it was a car she'd never seen before that day and never saw again after."

"Now's a good time to come forward with new information," Jordan grumbled.

"But it isn't new information," Scott said. "She told the exact same thing to the police when they interviewed her."

"There was nothing in the disclosure given to us by the D.A.'s office about a strange car," Sarajane said.

Jordan frowned. "She's right. Believe me—I would have jumped on something like that with both feet because there sure as hell wasn't anything more."

"That's what I figured," Scott said.

"You think the D.A.'s office buried it on purpose?" Sarajane asked.

"Wouldn't surprise me," Jordan said. "The whole damn trial was a mockery of the judicial system. As far as Judge Rhinehardt was concerned, Joe Juarez was guilty the moment those charges were laid.

"As for the A.D.A.," he continued, "well, there's a reason people call lawyers *sharks*. She scented blood on that first day and went straight for the kill."

Anyone else listening to Jordan rant about the blatant miscarriage of justice might have thought he was making excuses for losing the case—and his first. But Scott had read the trial transcripts, and he knew it was as bad as Joe's attorney described.

"But there are rules about disclosure," Sarajane protested. Then she brightened. "Hey, could this be grounds for an appeal?"

"Hard to say without knowing exactly what information wasn't disclosed," Jordan told her. Then to Scott, "You going to take a trip to the D.A.'s office?"

"That's my next stop," he confirmed.

Then he finished his coffee and went to have a chat with his ex-girlfriend.

Scott didn't call first.

He figured if Janie wasn't in her office, he'd just try again later, but he wanted to preserve the element of surprise.

As it turned out, he did catch her at her desk. And though she was surprised to see him, she didn't seem displeased, only a little wary.

"You haven't been here in more than two years," she said. "So I have to admit I'm curious about your reasons for coming here now."

"I want to discuss the Joe Juarez trial," he said.

"I guess I should have expected that after seeing you with his sister the other night."

He ignored the reference to Alicia. "Ethel Harbison gave a statement to the police—I wanted to know what was in their follow-up report."

"Scott, I have thirty-seven cases on this desk that are all ongoing. I don't have time to rehash old ones."

"She claimed she saw an unfamiliar vehicle parked

across the street from the Juarez residence the day the engine and plans went missing."

Janie stopped writing, glanced up. "And?"

"And I want to know why this information wasn't given to the defense."

"Because it was irrelevant."

"That wasn't your decision to make."

"Of course it was. The police took her statement. They investigated. Turned out the car belonged to a friend of the guy who lives across the street. In the house it was actually parked in front of and not across from. Therefore, the information was of absolutely no help to the defense and I wasn't obligated to provide it."

"Made sure your ass was covered on that one, did you?"

She narrowed her eyes at him. "Are you finished here?"

He mentally berated himself for not responding more diplomatically. The last thing he'd wanted was to antagonize her, especially when he needed her help. But he'd been as disappointed as he was surprised by her admission that she'd deliberately withheld the information.

"What happened to you, Janie?" he asked more softly. "You never used to take shortcuts. There was a time when you would have given the defense everything and been prepared to battle it out, to let the jury decide. It used to be that you believed in justice."

Her eyes were more weary than angry when they met his now. "It used to be that you did, too."

"You're right," he agreed. "And maybe I lost some of that faith when Freddie's killer walked free."

"And maybe I got burned too many times by slick defense attorneys who used irrelevant information to confuse their juries. But even so, I go back into that courtroom every day."

"Looking for justice—or just another notch in the win column?"

"I do my job," she said pointedly. "And I know your girlfriend's upset that her brother's in jail, but that's what happens when someone breaks the law."

"I read the trial transcript," he told her. "Seemed to me that Judge Rhinehardt was gunning for Joe Juarez from the beginning."

"Another interpretation might be that his defense attorney was incompetent."

"Come on, Janie. You know Jordan Hall's reputation. And I'm sure you know the case was dumped on his desk less than forty-eight hours before it was scheduled to go to trial. It wasn't unreasonable for him to ask for a postponement—and it wouldn't have been unreasonable for him to get it."

"I can agree that Rhinehardt's refusal was a tough break for the defense," she said. "But it was a ruling that was completely within his discretion to make."

He could tell she was thinking about it now, though, and wondering.

"I want to see the statement and the follow-up report," he told her.

"I didn't have to give it to the defense and I certainly don't have to give it to you."

"No, you don't," he agreed. "But I'm asking you to anyway. Please."

She sighed as she picked up her phone, buzzed her secretary. "Donna, can you dig out the Juarez file. Joe—grand larceny—trial was in…" She frowned.

"March," Scott supplied.

"Trial was in March," Janie said. "Thanks."

She replaced the receiver and turned back to him. "It's a fairly recent case so she shouldn't have to dig too far into the basement to find it."

"I appreciate it, Janie."

She shrugged off his gratitude.

"I did my job," she said again. "And you won't find anything that suggests otherwise."

While Scott was waiting for Donna to find the file, he went across the street to the deli to grab a sandwich. He brought back a sandwich for Janie, too, since it didn't seem as though she intended to take a break from her work anytime soon for lunch.

"Peace offering," he said, setting the tuna on whole wheat and a root beer on the corner of her desk.

"Thanks," she said absently, then she noticed the can and smiled. "I can't believe you remembered."

"It hasn't really been that long."

"More than two years since I left, and things were rocky long before that." She unwrapped her sandwich, took a bite. "I owe you an apology."

"For what?"

"Bailing on our relationship when you were at such a low point in your life."

He shrugged. "I know I made it difficult for you to want to stay."

"You're not holding a grudge?"

"As you said, it was more than two years ago."

"Yeah, but maybe I want to explain, to ease my own conscience."

"Okay."

"I blamed you for checking out of our relationship," she admitted. "But the truth is that you were lost after Freddie was killed and I didn't know how to bring you back. I didn't know how to help you, so I blamed you, instead. And then I cut my losses.

"I still think that what I did was the right thing for both of us. I couldn't give you what you needed. But maybe Alicia can."

"How does she figure into this?"

"You came charging in here today with fire in your eyes and guns blazing, showing a passion for life that you'd lost before I left. Maybe it's the passing of time that caused these changes—a natural part of the healing process. Or maybe it's her."

"And maybe you're reading too much into a three-minute meeting."

She smiled. "It scares you, doesn't it? Opening up your heart again. Maybe even falling in love again."

"It's not like that," he insisted.

"It's exactly like that," she said. "And if you took some time figuring out what to do about it instead of running away from it, you might even be happy again."

"I am happy," he said, and realized, for the first time in a long time, it was true.

"Then hold on to it. Hold on to her."

But Scott wasn't sure that he could, even if he wanted to.

And he was relieved when a brisk knock on the door prevented the conversation from going any further.

Donna came into the room, handed Janie the file.

"Thanks." She waited until the secretary had left the office, then passed it back across the desk to Scott.

"If you want copies of anything, I can do that," she said. "But the originals have to stay here."

He nodded, and she went back to her own work while he turned his attention to the file.

Janie had always been organized, so he wasn't surprised to find that there was an itemized list of the contents stapled inside the front cover. He scanned the list and sure enough, found Ethel Harbison's name.

> *18. Ethel Harbison—contact information p. 41*
> *19. Harbison—interview by Cst. Morrow pp. 42-44*
> *20. Harbison—statement　　　　　　　p. 45*

Scott flipped through the sequentially numbered pages to find Mrs. Harbison's statement, frowned when the numbers jumped from forty to forty-nine. He went back to the list of contents, reconfirmed the numbers of the pages he was looking for and noted the description of the others that were missing.

> *21. Byron Losani—contact information p. 46*
> *22. Losani—interview by Cst. Morrow　pp. 47-48*

Losani, he guessed, must be the neighbor from across the street, the one who claimed the vehicle had belonged to a friend of his.

But where was his statement?

Scott hunkered down over the file, scrutinized the contents.

"I can't find pages forty-one through forty-nine," he finally told Janie.

She frowned, but her fingers continued to click away on her keyboard. "They're probably just out of order."

"That's what I thought," he said. "But I've been through the whole folder."

She turned away from the computer to reach for the file.

He watched as she went through the same process he had just completed, watched as confusion slowly gave way to disbelief and then panic as she realized what he'd been trying to tell her.

The pages were missing.

Alicia approached Just Chillin' Salon & Spa with the same sense of trepidation she'd felt the first time she'd been here. Not that she didn't trust Aster completely—especially after the makeover that had made such a positive impression on both Scott and Joey. She just wondered about Lia's reaction to the vibrant woman, worried that the little girl might unintentionally insult Aster.

And as the first time she'd stood on the sidewalk, the door was pushed open from within and Aster stepped out.

"Are you just loiterin' on the sidewalk or you plannin' to come in?" she asked.

Alicia couldn't help but smile. "We're planning to come in, if you're not too busy."

But Lia was frowning at the other woman. "You have pink hair."

"It's the special today," Aster said solemnly. "Aren't you here to get pink hair, too?"

Lia shook her head. "But you could make my toenails pink."

"Toenails, huh?" Aster pretended to think this over.

"It was a half day at school today," Lia told her. "And Joey got to go to a friend's house, so Aunt Alicia said maybe we could do something special and we came here to have pet-a-cures."

"That sounds like something really special to me." Aster then dropped her voice, as if sharing a secret. "But I can't give you a pedicure out here on the sidewalk—municipal bylaws and all."

Lia nodded solemnly and followed Aster inside.

Alicia trailed after them, marveling at the ease with which her niece had taken to the other woman—pink hair notwithstanding.

"By the way, I'm Aster."

"I'm Lia."

"Lia the ballerina?" Aster asked.

Her niece smiled and nodded. "How did you know?"

"I've heard all about you," Aster said.

The little girl's eyes widened.

Aster nodded. "Mr. Logan told me about you—said you were the prettiest ballerina on stage the night he saw you dance."

"He brought me flowers," Lia said. "Tulips."

"Well, I should think so," Aster said, sliding a footbath into position for Alicia. "The star of the show should always have flowers."

As Alicia slipped her feet into the warm water she heard her niece giggle—a sound that had been all too rare in the past few weeks.

"And a ballerina should always take care of her feet," Aster said, carrying over a second footbath.

She helped Lia remove her shoes and socks, then

rolled up her pant legs so the little girl could soak her feet as her aunt was doing.

"Can I get you a juice box?" Aster asked Lia. "We have apple or fruit punch."

"Fruit punch," Lia said. "Please."

"One fruit punch comin' up." Aster turned to Alicia. "Coffee? Tea? Wine?"

"Coffee, please," Alicia said. "Black."

"All right," Aster said. "You ladies just relax, I'll be right back."

She finished Lia's pedicure, then gave the child a coloring book and box of crayons while she worked on Alicia's feet.

"I saw your P.I. this mornin'," Aster told her.

Alicia wanted to say that he wasn't *hers* but knew Aster wouldn't pay any attention to her protests.

"He was at the diner, ravin' about someone else's oatmeal chocolate chip cookies. Really riled Darlene."

"My neighbor's cookies," Alicia explained. "She seems to have a soft spot for him."

"Can't imagine a woman who wouldn't," the salon owner agreed. "But I think he was even more pleased about their conversation than the cookies. He was definitely pumped to check on the information she gave him."

"Hmm," was all Alicia said, having absolutely no idea what the woman was talking about.

"Not that he divulged any of the details," Aster hastened to assure her. "But he seemed to think he might finally have caught a break on your brother's case."

Scott's first impression of Constable Morrow was that the kid seemed barely old enough to shave. He had wide blue eyes, a quick smile, and the energy and enthusiasm of a cop who hadn't been on the job long enough to know any better.

But Scott was pleased to learn that the young cop also had a very sharp mind and was able to give a thorough rundown of his part of the Juarez investigation with barely a glance at his notes.

"I interviewed Losani twice," he told Scott. "First was during the initial canvass of the neighborhood. You know the usual questions—*were you home? did you see anything? hear anything?*—and so on. Losani said he'd been home all weekend but hadn't seen or heard anything. I didn't even get a statement from him first time out because he had nothing.

"Then Ethel Harbison tells me about this car— parked right in front of Losani's house, she said. And so we start asking other neighbors about it, a few confirm her description, and Losani calls me back—out of the blue—to tell me that this car belonged to a friend of his who was visiting from out of town."

"Are you sure he said *friend?*"

"Well, let me check now." And he flipped back through his notes, nodded. "A friend from Sacramento. John Roberts."

"What was your impression of Losani?" Scott pressed.

Morrow shrugged. "I have to admit, he didn't really make one when I did the initial interview. When he called me about the car, I didn't even recognize the name. Had to check back in my notes to be sure that I was the one who'd talked to him.

"The second time was pretty much the same as the

first, but I remember thinking that he seemed nervous. Of course, most people are when they talk to the cops."

"And what would you think if I told you that I had a conversation with Byron Losani this afternoon and he told me that the vehicle in question belonged to a cousin named Jack Richards."

The young cop scratched his head. "I'd have to think Mr. Losani was lying to one of us."

He nodded. "Which leads me to think that vehicle was more important than anyone believed."

Morrow couldn't deny the possibility, and Scott left the diner more convinced than ever that Joe Juarez had taken the fall for someone else. He still didn't know who or why, but he wasn't going to stop digging until he'd uncovered the truth.

He checked his cell phone for messages on the way home, smiled when he heard Alicia's voice.

"I know you said you had a meeting," she said. "But I wasn't sure if you'd have a chance to grab dinner. We had roast beef tonight and there are leftovers if you want to come by. If not, maybe I'll see you tomorrow."

That was it—end of message.

No pressure, no expectations, just "if you want to come by."

The problem was, he did want—maybe too much.

It scares you, doesn't it?

It was Janie's voice that echoed in his mind now, Janie's voice that forced him to face the truth that was staring him in the face.

Opening up your heart...falling in love again...you might even be happy again.

Maybe—or maybe he was a fool to even consider the

possibility of a future with Alicia. She was a forever kind of woman and he was a one-night-at-a-time kind of man. And yet, she was the woman he couldn't stop thinking about, couldn't stop wanting. And when he imagined his future, he couldn't imagine it without her.

The irony was that Alicia didn't seem to expect or even want anything more than what they had right now, and he was the one who had to keep reminding himself not to get caught up in dreams that would only come back and bite him in the ass.

So despite her offer of dinner and his own desire to see her, he stayed in the center lane and proceeded straight through the intersection, just to prove that he could. Just to prove to himself that he wouldn't be suckered in by a warm smile that was as innocent as it was seductive.

Hell, who was he kidding?

He made an illegal U-turn in the middle of the street.

Chapter Twelve

While Scott was asking Constable Morrow about Byron Losani, Alicia was asking some questions of her own—and she wasn't too pleased with the answers. Or maybe it was more accurate to say she wasn't pleased that Scott hadn't been the one to give her the answers.

"I can't believe he didn't tell me any of this," she said.

Mrs. H. nudged the plate of brownies closer to Alicia. "I'm sure he had his reasons."

She frowned as she selected a thick square with chocolate frosting and chopped walnuts sprinkled on top. "I hired him," Alicia reminded her. "He's supposed to report to me."

Mrs. H. sipped the herbal tea Alicia had made for her. "And I'm sure he will when he feels that he has something to report," she said soothingly. "He probably just didn't want to get your hopes up."

"But hope is all I've got right now," Alicia told her.

"Hope…and a hunky P.I. keeping your bed warm," Mrs. H. said.

Alicia felt her cheeks flame.

"And there's nothing wrong with that," her neighbor hurried to reassure her. "I might be of a different generation, but I'm no prude. And you're a beautiful young woman who deserves to have some joy in her life."

"We were talking about my brother," Alicia reminded her.

"No, you were prying for information about my conversation with Mr. Logan."

"Only because he didn't tell me himself."

"Did he tell you he was going to see Byron Losani today?"

Alicia shook her head.

"Well, his car was parked across the street about two o'clock this afternoon—in the exact same spot I saw that other car the day that stuff was stolen from your brother's house.

"He wasn't there very long," the older woman continued. "Maybe half an hour or so. But what I thought was even more interesting was the other vehicle that was parked there later. A small SUV, California plates."

She pulled a scrap of paper out of her pocket, passed it across the table to Alicia. "This time, I got the license plate number."

Scott's heart slammed into his throat when he turned onto Greenleaf Drive and spotted the flashing lights.

There were police cars and fire trucks and an ambulance, and the emergency vehicles were blocking the street right in front of the Juarez house.

With a squeal of tires, he pulled over to the curb, slammed out of his car and raced toward the house.

Alicia was on the porch, and he almost collapsed with relief when he saw her there. For a minute he'd thought—

No. He shoved aside the initial panic, the heart-stopping terror, and concentrated on breathing. She was okay.

He exhaled a shaky breath and slowed his pace.

Mrs. H. was with her, he saw now, and they were watching the house across the street.

Byron Losani's house, where the front door was wide-open and the lights were blazing inside.

The overpowering relief he felt upon seeing that Alicia was okay was nudged aside by a growing trepidation that Losani was not.

As he got closer to the Juarez house, he saw Mrs. H. stand up. She patted Alicia's shoulder, waved an acknowledgment in his direction, and crossed the driveway to her own home.

He wanted to haul Alicia into his arms, to hold her tight, to let the warmth of her battle back the lingering vestiges of his fear. Instead, he lowered himself to the step beside her, so they were sitting thigh to thigh, shoulder to shoulder, and turned his head to touch his lips lightly to hers. "Hey."

"Hey, yourself." Her posture was stiff, her eyes still fixed on the house across the street. "There's been more excitement in this neighborhood in the past three months than the three years before that."

"Any idea what's going on?"

She shook her head. "I was in the kitchen with Mrs. H. when we heard the sirens."

She fell silent, and he knew it wasn't just because her attention was focused on the action at Losani's house.

"You're mad at me," he guessed.

"Don't you think I have reason to be?" she challenged. "I found out about your conversation with Mrs. H. from Aster."

"Aster?" He couldn't have been more surprised if she'd said it was posted on a billboard downtown.

"Yes, when Lia and I went for pedicures today."

"I didn't tell Aster anything," he protested.

"Maybe you didn't give her any details, but you gave her more information than you gave me."

He sighed. "Okay, you're entitled to be upset. But you could at least give me a chance to explain."

"I don't need an explanation—I need you to be honest with me."

"Okay," he said again, and proceeded to tell her everything he'd learned in his meetings with Jordan, Janie, Losani and Morrow.

"Mrs. H. told me she saw your car across the street today," she told him.

"And if I'd been trying to hide my visit to Mr. Losani, I wouldn't have parked where I knew she would see my vehicle."

Alicia nodded and pulled a piece of paper out of her pocket. "Someone else wasn't so smart."

"What's this?"

"The license plate number of another vehicle that she saw parked in the same spot a few hours later."

He slipped the paper into his own pocket.

"You talked to Mr. Losani, then someone else dropped by for a visit, and now this," she murmured, her eyes once again focused on the chaos across the street.

"We don't know what *this* is," he pointed out cautiously.

"No," she agreed. "But it's a strange coincidence, don't you think?"

"Yeah." He slid his arm over her shoulders, pulled her closer.

This time she curled into him willingly, then whispered, "I'm scared."

He didn't know how to respond to that admission, except to hold her tighter.

And he knew, when he saw them carry out Losani's body on a stretcher, she had every reason to be.

Alicia had done a lot of thinking after Scott left and was feeling a little better for it when she woke up in the morning. She didn't want to believe the attack on Byron Losani could be linked to the events that had sent her brother to prison, but there was no denying that the situation had started to escalate as soon as Scott began to uncover minor inconsistencies and questionable circumstances surrounding Joe's arrest and trial.

A few months earlier, she hadn't thought anything could be worse than her brother being arrested for a crime she knew he didn't commit. Now a man had been brutally beaten, possibly for no other reason than that he'd given a false alibi to whomever had set up her brother.

And for what?

She still didn't understand the importance of the prototype and the plans. Joe had told her it was cutting-edge technology that would revolutionize the racing industry, put Russo's Dirt Devils on the front pages and reap financial benefits for everyone involved in the project when it was finally unveiled. Now it was gone.

The engine design was supposed to have been a secret—no one outside of the team was to know of its existence. Of course, some people couldn't resist talking, especially when they had bragging rights to something so big.

But she still didn't understand how someone could benefit from stealing the plans. It made sense that Russo's competitors would be interested in the technology, but if another team showed up on the circuit with a similarly designed engine, it would be obvious where the missing plans had gone.

Which brought her back full circle to the question of who would profit from the theft.

She gave up trying to figure out the who and the why and resolved to let the police put all the pieces together. She would concentrate on her brother. Because she was more convinced than ever that Joe still had at least some of those pieces, and she wasn't going to let him hold on to them any longer. And after clearing it with her supervisor to take a couple of hours off, she dialed Scott's number.

If he was surprised by her call, he didn't let on. And he didn't hesitate when she asked him to go with her to the prison. Less than half an hour later, they were on their way.

He made conversation while he drove, talking to her about everything from the highlights of the previous night's baseball game to Aster's new hair color— burgundy—which he'd seen when he stopped at the diner to pick up coffee for them both. She appreciated the effort he was making to keep her mind off the impending confrontation with her brother, even if it was futile.

By the time he'd passed through the security gate and pulled into the parking lot, worry and anticipation were a hard knot deep in her belly.

"Are we going to play good cop/bad cop?" He took her hand to lead her toward the entrance.

She managed to smile, because she knew that was what he wanted her to do. "Maybe later, if you bring the handcuffs."

"I might be able to find a pair that I kept as a souvenir from my old job."

"Promises, promises."

He chuckled and squeezed her hand gently. "Are you sure you want to do this?"

"I'm sure that I don't have any other choice. I need answers, and I'm more convinced than ever that Joe's the only one who can give them to me."

"Then I'll let you take the lead," he said. "He is, after all, your brother."

"Okay."

He tipped her chin up, kissed her softly.

And the tenderness of the unexpected gesture helped take the sharpest edge off of her nerves.

"Scott."

"Yeah?"

"Thank you."

He smiled. "Let's get this done."

The farther they moved away from the doors and into the prison, the tenser Alicia got. Scott could see it in the stiffness of her shoulders and the set of her jaw.

He wanted, more than anything, to take her worries away and make everything right in her world again.

And then what?

Then she wouldn't need him anymore. Joe would go back home to be with his family, Alicia would return to her own apartment and her own life—working at the clinic, taking her classes, dreaming of a family. And his life would be as empty as it was before he met her.

Not an appealing scenario from his perspective, but still one he would give to her if he could.

But first they had to get some answers from Joe.

"Who is Jack Richards?" Alicia asked the question before Joe had even sat down.

Her brother's face remained blank as he settled into the chair across from her. "Who?"

The question was asked casually. Almost too casually, Scott thought. With just the right amount of disinterest to be anything less than deliberate.

"Byron Losani gave that name to Scott. A few hours later, he was beaten unconscious."

"Beaten?" Joe sounded surprised, but not shocked.

And Scott suspected that Alicia's brother had already heard about Losani's misfortune. Information like that, he knew, traveled quickly behind prison walls—especially when there was a point being made.

"Did Jack Richards do it?" she asked.

"I don't know."

"Okay, let's try something else…" she said "…555-4393."

"Your high school locker combination?" he guessed.

"You know, this attitude of yours is really starting to piss me off, Joe."

"And yours is starting to piss me off," her brother

said. "I've already been through a police investigation and a trial. I don't need you coming in here and interrogating me."

"I'm trying to help you!"

"I didn't ask for your help!"

Scott reached under the table and laid his hand on Alicia's knee, squeezed gently. Screw prison protocol, he thought. Because if he didn't intervene and somehow calm her down, they were both going to get tossed out.

Thankfully, she seemed to understand his unspoken warning and she paused to take a deep breath, then slowly released it.

"You're right," she said finally. "You didn't ask for help. But I'm not going to sit back and let you spend the next five years of your life in prison just because you're too stubborn to ask."

"And don't you think that if I knew anything that would help get me out of here and home safe with my family, I would tell you?"

"I don't know what to think anymore," she said, frustration creeping back into her voice.

"The number Alicia recited is a phone number," Scott interjected. "From which several calls were made to your house."

"Probably a wrong number," Joe said dismissively. "You wouldn't believe how many of those I get at home."

"Except that one of the calls lasted seventeen minutes, another was twelve minutes, and a third was almost twenty minutes," she pointed out.

"Hell, Ali. I don't know. Maybe he was selling something and I couldn't get him off the line."

"*She*," Alicia corrected.

"What?"

"Scott traced the cell phone number back to a woman named Elaine Nomolos."

"If you knew that, why did you bother asking me whose number it was?"

"Because Elaine Nomolos doesn't exist. But it just so happens that Nomolos is Solomon spelled backwards. And Elaine is Lia's middle name, which she was given because it's also her mother's middle name."

Joe actually laughed, which Scott could tell really irritated Alicia.

"Yvette can't even afford a hot meal, never mind a cell phone."

"But she's capable of filling out the registration information and buying it for someone else, isn't she?"

"Except that Yvette doesn't do anything for anyone else without a reason," Joe reminded her.

"You're protecting her," Alicia accused. "Just like you've always protected her."

Joe didn't say anything, but the muscle in his jaw flexed as he clenched his teeth together.

"Is she really more important to you than Joey and Lia?" his sister demanded. "Is she more important than I am?"

"Damn you, Ali." His eyes shone with angry tears. "You know nothing is more important to me than my family—and that's Joey and Lia and you before anyone else."

"Then why?" she demanded.

"*Because* nothing is more important to me than my family."

And he pushed away from the table and walked back to the guard.

Alicia sat there for several minutes after he'd been escorted from the room.

Then she stood up and turned away, striding across the room in the opposite direction her brother had taken. Scott followed silently. He knew her well enough now to recognize the temper that was simmering, and to understand the hurt that had caused it.

"If he's protecting her, after everything she did to screw up his life, then he deserves to spend the next five years locked up in here," she said at last.

"It's human nature to protect those we love," he told her. "And even if he isn't in love with her anymore, she's still the mother of his children."

"Children who are now living without their mother *or* their father because he's in prison." She waited for the buzzer to release the door, then pushed through to the outdoors and into the sunshine. "God, I hate that place."

He followed her across the parking lot. "I can understand why you're upset, but I can't condemn your brother. Even if he's doing the wrong thing, he believes he's doing it for the right reasons."

"Then he's an idiot," she said succinctly. "And I can't believe you're taking his side.

"I'm not taking his side."

"Or maybe I can," she continued, as if he hadn't spoken. "Because you did exactly the same thing, didn't you? All along, you've been keeping information about the investigation from me, even though I'm the one who hired you to find the truth."

"I didn't want you to be disappointed if the evidence I'd found didn't lead anywhere."

"You were trying to protect me," she said disdainfully. "The big strong man looking out for the little woman who isn't capable of dealing with her own emotions."

"No," he denied. "Okay, yes. I was trying to protect you. But not for the reasons you think."

"Then why?" she demanded.

"Because you matter to me."

Alicia could only stare at him as the last of her self-righteous anger and indignation fizzled away.

"Oh…um…oh."

Scott gave her a crooked smile. "Yeah, I know. We were supposed to keep it simple, not tangle it up with messy emotions."

"Is it tangled?" she asked, half hopefully, half fearfully.

"It's starting to seem that way. I have feelings for you that I didn't expect to have—didn't want to have."

"Are you sorry?"

"I'm afraid I will be," he admitted. "Because I'm still not sure I can give you what you want. But we've got something started now, and I'd kind of like to see where it goes."

"I'd like to see where it goes, too," she said, working to keep her voice level and her feet on the ground while hope ballooned inside her chest.

It was hardly a declaration of undying love, and yet, his obvious reluctance to acknowledge the feelings he had for her gave her hope that those feelings might be deeper than he'd admitted to himself. But she wouldn't push for more than he was ready to give—not when he'd already given her more than she'd dreamed of. She would just savor those words for a while and hope that maybe, just maybe, he might grow to love her someday.

In the meantime, she was standing in the prison parking lot, staring at him across the hood of his car, torn between her hopes for a future with this man and her concerns about the future for her brother.

"But right now, we need to go back," she said. "The kids will be getting home from school soon."

Alicia and Scott got back to Joe's house just as the school bus was arriving. Just in time to see Lia race up the driveway, her eyes wide and full of tears. And the uneasiness that had been gnawing inside Alicia's belly all day suddenly grabbed hold with sharp fangs.

"What's wrong, Lia?"

The little girl sobbed. "I told him not to go. I told him, but he didn't listen to me. He never listens to me."

She immediately knew who the *him* was because Joey hadn't followed his sister off the bus as he usually did. "Where did he go?"

"He asked me not to tell. He made me promise."

"But you're worried about him, aren't you?"

Lia sniffled and nodded.

"A promise is important," she told her niece. "But it's also important to do what feels right in your heart, and you should never keep a secret that makes you uncomfortable."

"He went to the racetrack," Lia said. "He told me he had money for the city bus and said he would be home for dinner, so I shouldn't tell you that he'd gone. But the racetrack's far away and Daddy doesn't work there anymore, so I don't think he should have gone all by himself."

"No," Alicia said, carefully controlling her own worry and fear so as not to upset her niece any further. "He shouldn't have. And you were right to tell me, even though Joey asked you not to."

"Are you going to go get him?" Lia asked worriedly.

Alicia nodded. "Yes, I'll go get him."

"We'll go get him," Scott said, touching a hand to her arm.

For a moment, she'd almost forgotten he was there. And though she was used to handling family crises on her own, she was grateful for his presence and relieved that she wasn't on her own this time. So she took Lia over to Mrs. Harbison's and gave the neighbor a quick summary of the situation before climbing back into the passenger seat of Scott's car.

She was quiet through most of the drive to the racetrack, thinking, worrying. She could tell by Scott's silence and his white-knuckled grip on the steering wheel that he was worried, too.

He'd said that she mattered to him, but she knew Joey and Lia mattered to him, too. Probably more than he realized, and certainly more than he would have expected in only the few weeks he'd been coming around her brother's house. It made her wonder why he was so adamantly opposed to having a family of his own, and immediately reproach herself for wondering. Right now, Joey was all that mattered.

She tried to focus on the traffic and not to count the minutes or speculate about her nephew's motivations for taking off, but she couldn't shut off her mind.

Had someone at school said something to upset him? She knew some of the kids liked to make nasty remarks about Joe being in prison, but Joey usually managed to ignore them.

Had he remembered something he'd left at the track on his last visit to his father's work? If he had, she would have expected he would ask her to take him back to get it.

Or maybe he'd just been missing Joe and wanted to go to the place where they'd shared so many happy memories. She could see why a boy who had trouble expressing his feelings might want to make that kind of journey on his own. She didn't approve, but she could understand.

Finally Scott pulled into the parking lot.

"There's no one here," he noted.

"It's Tuesday," she reminded him. "There are only races on the weekends."

But the quiet and emptiness were unnerving. Other than a few trailers with team logos on their sides and a pickup truck with two flat tires, the lot was empty. But somewhere out there, somewhere in the vast space of the racetrack, was her nephew, and she had to find him.

She was reaching for the door handle before Scott had even turned off the engine.

"Wait." He put a hand on her arm. "This place is too big to go tearing off without a plan."

"I have a plan," she said. "Find him, kick his butt and go home."

He nodded. "Okay, but with one addition—we stick together."

"We'll find him quicker if we split up."

"Maybe. But then we'd waste time looking for one another." He unlocked his glove box, pulled out a gun.

Alicia drew in a startled breath. "What's that for?"

"Just a precaution," he assured her, and he gave the weapon a quick check before tucking it into his pocket.

"You have a strange feeling about this, too, don't you?"

"Let's not speculate about anything right now. Just stick with me, okay?"

"Okay."

"I told Lia we would find him together," he reminded her. "And we will."

She slipped her hand into the one he held out to her and let herself be comforted by his touch and his words.

They walked through the main gates, started around the track.

"He was wearing jeans," she told Scott, trying to picture him as he'd sat at the table eating his cereal that morning. "And a gray T-shirt. But he took his jacket, too. It's red. If he's wearing that, he should be easy to spot."

She was nervous, babbling. Her emotions were a tangled mass knotted deep in her belly. Worry. Anger. Frustration. Fear.

Where the hell was he?

"Joey!" she called out.

There was no response except from Scott, who squeezed her hand reassuringly.

"Joey!"

She looked up at the stands. They were open and empty, and she didn't see anyone, not even a maintenance worker or security person, around.

But Scott started up the metal steps anyway. "We'll have a better view of the grounds from the top."

"Joey!"

The fear was growing with every step she took,

every call that went unanswered, but she battled it back. Her nephew knew his way around here probably better than she did. He was likely just hiding out somewhere, listening to his iPod, and couldn't hear her calling to him. And when she found him, she was taking the damned iPod away and grounding him for a month.

When she found him...

She closed her eyes and sent up a quick prayer that it would be soon.

But as they neared the top of the structure, her doubts took firmer hold. It was obvious he wasn't hanging around any of his usual places, possible he wasn't even there anymore. "Maybe he already went home," she said.

"Mrs. H. said she'd call my cell phone if he turned up," Scott reminded her.

She nodded and called out again. "Joey!"

"Wait." Scott stopped. "What was that?"

Alicia halted beside him and fell silent, listening.

Then she heard it, too, a knocking sound coming from the announcer's box at the top of the next seating section.

Scott was already taking the last steps two at a time, then racing toward the boxes.

"He's here." Scott vaulted over the desktop and into the box.

Her relief, so overwhelming she nearly sank to the ground, was short-lived. Because when she entered the booth through the door, she saw that Joey was there—bound and gagged.

"Oh, Joey." She fell to her knees beside the chair to which he was tied and immediately started to unfasten the gag. His eyes were swimming with tears, his cheeks streaked with evidence of others he'd already shed, and she felt dangerously close to crying herself.

While she went to work on the knot at the back of his head, her fingers trembling and fumbling, Scott got started on the ropes at his feet.

Joey was crying again, big tears that tracked down his face and silent sobs that shook his slender shoulders. She wanted to hold him, to pull him in her lap and comfort him as she had when he was a child. But he wasn't a child anymore, as evidenced by this very adult mess he'd wandered into.

As they untied him, Joey explained how he'd ended up there.

Apparently he'd gone to play pinball at lunch and ran into someone at the restaurant who claimed to know his father. More importantly, the man claimed to have information about the stolen plans and proof that Joe hadn't taken them. But he would only give that proof to Joey, and only if he went to the track alone.

And, of course, that was the one thing that would entice Joey to disobey everything he knew to be smart and right and go tearing off to the racetrack on his own.

"Oh, Joey." She stroked a hand over his hair, her heart aching for the boy who so desperately needed the answers she'd also been seeking.

Scott moved away from them after Joey was freed and stood looking out at the track. His hand was in his pocket—the same pocket where he'd put his gun. She knew he was searching for the man who'd brought Joey here, wondering where he'd gone, when he'd be back.

"I was supposed to meet him at four-thirty," Joey

said. "But I caught a bus right after school, and I got here early, before he did, even. And I saw him meet up with someone else in the parking lot. It was dad's boss—Mr. Lawrence."

Scott's head swiveled around at that. "Did you hear what they said?"

"No. I was too far away. But I saw Mr. Lawrence give the other guy a bag. Then Jack—that's what the other guy said his name was—tossed it into his trunk of his car."

"Did Jack give you his last name?"

"Yeah—it was Richards."

"Jack Richards," Alicia whispered.

Joey frowned. "Do you know him?"

"No," she said.

And Scott asked, "What happened next?"

"I met him at the main gate at four-thirty, like he told me to. When I asked for the proof he'd promised me, he brought me up here and—" he looked away, his eyes filling with tears again "—he tied me up."

"And just left you here?"

"He stayed for a while," Joey told them. "Watching for you. When your car pulled into the parking lot, he said it was time for him to go."

"None of this is making any sense to me," she said.

"I don't get it, either," Scott admitted. "Was there anything else he said to you, Joey?"

The boy hesitated and sent a worried glance in her direction. She forced a smile, trying to reassure her nephew despite her growing trepidation.

"What did he say to you?" she prompted gently.

"He didn't say anything else. But he, uh, he gave me a note. To give to you."

He took a crumpled piece of paper from his pocket and handed it to Alicia.

She unfolded it with trembling fingers.

You must be greatly relieved to find your nephew unharmed. Next time, you won't be so lucky. And neither will he. Or maybe it will be his little sister who pays if you don't back off.

She handed the note to Scott without a word, unable to speak around the terror that choked her throat.

She'd never understood why her brother had willingly gone to prison for a crime he didn't commit—until now. Now she knew that Joe had gone to jail to keep his children safe. And, heaven help her, Alicia would let him stay in jail for the same reason.

"I'm really sorry." Joey's voice broke. "I know I shouldn't have come out here on my own. I just really wanted to hear what he knew about Dad."

"I know, Joe." Alicia hugged him tight, her heart aching with relief that her nephew was okay and breaking at the realization that his father's fate was now sealed. She would fight any enemy against impossible odds for her brother, but she wouldn't do anything that would put his children in danger.

"Then you're not mad?" he asked hopefully.

"Oh, I'm mad," she assured him. "It just so happens that my relief is outweighing the mad right now. But you're definitely grounded."

His face fell. "For how long?"

"At least a year."

"A year?"

She forced a smile. "Ask me tomorrow when my heart is beating normally again and you might get a different answer, okay?"

"Okay," Joey agreed, and let her put her arm around him.

"Let's get both of you home," Scott said.

Alicia fought back tears as she nodded and followed him out of the press box.

She was overwhelmingly and indescribably grateful that Joey was safe, but she was also devastated by the realization that her brother wouldn't be home for another five years. How would he survive that time in prison? And how would she manage to let the children out of her sight for even a minute after what had happened today?

How could she let them get on the school bus in the morning and not worry about all the horrible things that could happen in the hours that she was away from them? How could she possibly pretend life was normal with such a threat hanging over all of their heads?

She glanced up and saw that there was, in fact, an ominous dark cloud ahead.

Smoke, she realized, as the acrid scent registered in her mind along with the chemical odor of something that might have been gasoline.

"Something's burning," she said.

Scott looked up at the sky, then started to run toward the parking lot.

Alicia and Joey followed, racing around the corner just in time to watch Scott's vintage Corvette explode in a terrifyingly glorious display of flames.

Chapter Thirteen

Scott gave his statement to Constable Morrow, clearly and concisely detailing every step of the incident, focusing on the events as if he'd observed them from a distance and ignoring the emotions that continued to churn violently inside of him.

Alicia hadn't wanted him to mention Jack Richards's name, and he understood why. She was afraid the man would follow through on his threats to harm Joey or Lia—or both—if she didn't back off. But Scott couldn't lie about what had happened, and he didn't want to. Alicia believed her brother's children would be safe if she stopped digging into the events that had led Joe to prison, but Scott knew they wouldn't ever truly be safe until Jack Richards was behind bars.

Richards had proven his ruthlessness by terrorizing a twelve-year-old boy who wanted only to believe in the innocence of his father, and Scott wasn't going to let him get away with that. The torching of his 'Vette had seemed insignificant in comparison to what might have happened to Joey—until the car exploded and Alicia went down.

She'd taken an instinctive step back, away from the heat and flames that shot out from the fireball, and lost her footing.

He'd seen her out of the corner of his eye, had watched it happen as if in slow motion. He'd tried to reach for her, but he was too far away, couldn't seem to move fast enough. And he'd watched, helplessly, as she fell backward to the ground.

She tried to twist around.

Her elbow hit the gravel; her head hit the curb.

It was a freaky accident—as unavoidable as it had been unpredictable. And as terrifying as anything he'd ever witnessed.

She'd lost consciousness only for a moment, but that moment had seemed like an eternity to Scott who held her while Joey called 9-1-1.

He could still feel the stickiness of her blood on his hands, could still feel the panic that had built inside of him until there was nothing else.

Then she'd moaned softly and her eyelids had flickered.

And the panic subsided, but somehow the terror remained.

He walked away from Constable Morrow, with only a glance toward the ambulance where Alicia was with the paramedics. He needed some space and some distance to breathe and think and get his feelings under control.

Because despite his outward calm, he was shaking.

His hands were unsteady, his insides were trembling. His stomach was pitching so badly he thought he was going to puke.

He could still see her lying there—pale, still, bleeding. And he'd thought she was dead. He'd thought he'd lost her, just like he'd lost Freddie.

No, it wasn't anything like when Freddie was killed. It was worse. So much worse.

Freddie had been his partner and his best friend. And when he'd died, his life draining away along with the blood that spilled out onto Scott's hands, something inside Scott had died, too.

He'd shut down after that. He'd went through the motions of life, but he hadn't really been living. In fact, he hadn't felt a damn thing for the longest time.

Not until Alicia.

Alicia had made him laugh and live and love.

Yeah—it had taken her being knocked unconscious for him to recognize the truth: he loved her.

Love hadn't been part of the plan, he'd been clear about that from the beginning. But somehow it had snuck up on him anyway, until he was so tangled up inside with feelings for her, he could hardly think.

He sure as hell wasn't thinking about anything else but her, and how close he might have come to losing her.

And it was too much.

He couldn't do it. He couldn't let himself experience that kind of emotion again. Where there was joy, there could be sorrow; where there was pleasure, there could be pain; where there was life, there could be death. With

Alicia, he could have everything—and he could lose everything.

And maybe he was a coward, but it was just too big a risk to take.

The paramedics wanted to take Alicia to the hospital, but she refused. She was a nurse, she explained to them, and could take care of herself. Besides, she needed to go home, to be close to Joey and Lia, to watch out for the children her brother had entrusted to her care. It was all she could do for them now.

The ambulance attendants weren't convinced, but once again, Scott came through for her, promising that he would call his brother—who was a doctor—to check her out, and then stay with her through the night.

And he did stay, but he didn't sleep with her.

Not that Alicia was in the mood for lovemaking, but she would have appreciated some cuddling. She wanted him beside her, his arms around her. But Scott insisted that she would rest better if she had the bed to herself, and he stayed in the chair by her side.

Physically, he was right there, doing exactly what he'd promised to do—keep an eye on her and watch out for the kids. But emotionally, he was already pulling away. She knew it was true even if she didn't understand why.

And when he picked up a detective novel she'd left on the bedside table and pretended to be reading, she turned so he wouldn't see the tears that spilled onto her cheeks as she silently cried herself to sleep.

Detective Rucynski came by in the morning to let them know that Jack Richards was in jail, thanks primarily to Joe's ex-wife. Apparently Yvette had panicked and called the police when she found a bag full of money and a picture of Joey in Jack's hotel room. Fearing for her son's safety, she'd willingly turned her lover in to the police and confessed her part in the crimes that had sent Joe to prison.

There were still some missing pieces, Rucynski told them, but the grand larceny investigation had been reopened and it looked like Joe would be coming home soon.

Alicia was thrilled for her brother, relieved that her family was safe, but miserably unhappy herself as she prepared to say goodbye to Scott.

He'd called a cab to take him into work as soon as Rucynski had gone, making it clear that he didn't intend to hang around and babysit her all day. Not that she needed a babysitter, of course. She just wanted to be with him. The events of the previous day had shaken her to the core and she just wanted to keep everyone she loved close to her.

But Scott had other plans and going into the office was at the top of his list.

She didn't know what to say to him, how to reach him, what had happened to make him pull away. And she was afraid there was nothing she could say, no words that would reach him, because he was already gone.

There was a beep from the driveway, and a peek out the front window confirmed that his cab had arrived.

"I have to go," he said.

She followed him to the door. "I don't know if I said this already, but I'm sorry about your car."

"My car?" He looked at her blankly.

"The classic Stingray that you spent eighteen months restoring," she reminded him.

"It was just a set of wheels," he said.

"Okay, if you're not upset about the 'Vette, what's going on?"

"What do you mean?"

"You've been stepping back from me since we were at the racetrack. No—not just stepping back, running away."

"I really don't think this is the right time for a dissertation about our relationship."

But she knew that if they didn't talk now, they might not have another chance. "Send the cab away," she suggested. "Stay awhile longer."

"I can't. I have a lot of work waiting for me at the office."

"And it has to be done today?"

"Yeah. I need to contact Jordan, too, so he can start the ball rolling to get your brother released from prison. That's what this was all about, wasn't it?"

The casual words and careless tone sliced through her like a blade.

"Not to me," she said softly.

He sighed heavily. "Don't do this, Alicia."

"Don't do what?" she demanded.

"Don't pretend this was ever any more than a temporary thing."

"Less than twenty-four hours ago, you told me that you wanted to see where our relationship was going."

"That was before I realized it wasn't going anywhere."

And that simply, her hopes and her heart shattered.

Alicia turned away. She wasn't going to beg. She wasn't going to throw away her pride along with her heart.

Then she thought, to hell with it, and she pivoted back on her heel.

"No," she decided. "I'm not going to make this easy

for you. I'm not going to let you walk away until you know exactly what you're walking away from."

"Alicia—"

"I didn't tell you this before—" she forged ahead as if he hadn't tried to interrupt "—because I didn't want to give you an excuse to panic and leave. But you don't need any help making excuses. You do that just fine on your own. So here it is— I love you, Scott."

She held up a hand to forestall the protest she knew would be coming. "I know it was against your so-called rules. I know I wasn't supposed to feel this way. And I didn't want to. But I can't turn my emotions on and off like a tap, and I'm not going to apologize for that.

"If I'm sorry about anything, it's that you can't see how good we were together, that you can't seem to appreciate the life we could have built together. And I hope that when you wake up one morning and think about what might have been, you'll remember that it was your choice, not mine."

Then she turned and walked away before he could.

Joe came home that night.

The police hadn't yet sorted out all the details with respect to the original charges against him, but there were enough that Jordan was able to get a court order for Joe's release pending the official reversal of his conviction.

Yvette was in rehab, which was a condition of her deal with the prosecution. She would also have to testify against Jack Richards at trial in exchange for a probationary sentence for her part in the crime.

Joe's ex-wife had been recruited by Jack to get Joe away from the house, which she'd done by showing up at the door and asking for cab fare to get her across town. Joey had been at soccer practice and Lia at ballet class, and Joe had been anxious to get rid of Yvette before they came home. But he worried any money he gave her might be used for drugs rather than transportation, so he drove her instead, as she'd figured he would, giving Jack the opportunity to get in to steal the engine and the plans.

Alicia wasn't too annoyed that her former sister-in-law was getting off with a slap on the wrist because her role had been minimal and because she didn't want the children to have their father released from prison only to have their mother confined.

Jack Richards, on the other hand, would be going away for a very long time. The list of charges facing him was long and diverse, ranging from the original theft to forcible confinement to the assault of Byron Losani. The evidence against him, Rucynski assured her, was solid.

Of course, Jack was a hired professional, and he was bargaining with everything he had to implicate the race team owners in order to cut the amount of time he would have to do in jail. The bag of money he'd received from Matt Lawrence Sr. was proof of his involvement, but the police still hadn't determined if Gene Russo was also mixed up in the scheme.

At least now they had a motive for the theft, which was what had stumped Alicia from the beginning. Although, not surprisingly, the motive was financial.

Apparently there were more problems with the engine design than the company had originally suspected, and while progress was being made, it wasn't happening quickly enough and there was concern that the funding from their sponsors would run out before the snags could be worked out. Of course, the prototype was insured, and while the theft of it would be a blow to the project, it would be a boon to the books.

Of course, Joe hadn't known all of this when he was arrested. He'd only known that Yvette had gotten herself tangled up with some guy who was threatening to hurt Joey and Lia if Joe didn't go along with his plan. From his perspective, he hadn't had any choice—he would do anything for his children.

And now that she knew all of the details, Alicia acknowledged to herself as she gathered her belongings in preparation to move back to her apartment, she could understand why he'd kept quiet.

She hadn't realized that Joey was also keeping quiet about something, too, until he came in to sit on the bed while she finished packing.

"Have you decided how long I'm grounded for?" he asked.

"Well, now that your dad's home, I think that's probably something you should work out with him," she said.

"Dad told me that it should be up to you, because what I did affected you most directly." He glanced away, and she knew it was so that she wouldn't see the tears that filled his eyes. "I'm really sorry you got hurt, Aunt Alicia."

She sat down beside him. "It wasn't your fault, Joey."

"There's something else I need to apologize for."

She waited.

"It's about Lia's lawn ornaments." He dropped his head. "I did it. I wrecked them. I didn't mean to do it," he hurried on. "And I wasn't trying to upset Lia. I was just so mad about everything and it felt good to break something. But then, afterward, I just felt bad."

"Did you tell your sister?" she asked.

He shook his head. "Not yet."

"You know that's what you need to do, don't you?"

"Yeah." He sighed. "But she's going to want to break something of mine."

"Do you think that's fair?" she asked.

"Probably," he admitted grudgingly. "But I've got money in my piggy bank—maybe I can bribe her instead."

"That's something the two of you can work out," she said.

"Is that going to add time to my grounding?"

"I don't think so. I'm not happy about what you did, but I'm proud of you for knowing that it was wrong and owning up to it."

"So how long am I grounded for?"

"A week without video games," she decided impulsively.

"A week?" he protested, then seemed to realize a week was a lot less than the year she'd threatened him with the day before. "A week seems fair."

She smiled. "But you still have to face your sister."

"Okay." He sighed as he slid off the edge of the bed and went to do just that.

It was almost six o'clock on Saturday night and Scott was at home listening to the message that had been left on his machine three days earlier. He couldn't count the number of times he'd replayed it in those three days, just to hear the sound of Alicia's voice.

It was pathetic, he knew, but it was all he had left. A

twelve-second message on a tape that he couldn't bear to erase because then he would have nothing.

It was his own fault; he knew that, too.

She'd offered him her heart, and he'd refused to accept it. Because it was easier to reject her than risk loving and losing her.

I love you, Scott.

The words echoed in his mind, but he rejected those, too.

If she really loved him, wouldn't she have fought for him to stay?

Your choice, she'd said.

And he knew that it would have to be.

He could stay here and be miserable and alone for the rest of his life, or he could take a chance that she'd meant what she said, that she did love him, and hope that they might build a future together.

But could he give her what she wanted?

Because if he couldn't, if he wanted her without being willing to offer marriage and the family he knew she wanted, then he was as selfish as Janie had once accused him of being.

He'd never seriously contemplated marriage before. He'd discussed it, in abstract terms, when he was living with Janie, but neither of them had wanted to make that kind of commitment.

And marriage was a commitment—a legally binding promise to share a life, for better or for worse, till death.

He couldn't deny that the death part rattled him. Freddie's murder had taught him some hard lessons about the precariousness of life that he never wanted to repeat again. And then there had been that brief, heart-stopping moment when he'd thought he might lose Alicia, too.

In the past couple of years, he hadn't wanted anything that hinted at permanence or obligation. And the suggestion of marriage rattled him enough without adding the possibility of children into the mix.

True, he'd really taken to Jake's twin toddlers and LJ's new son, Liam. And though he'd felt a little awkward with Joey and Lia at first, he'd got to the point where he actually enjoyed being with them.

Still, the idea of being a father, of having kids of his own, was terrifying…and intriguing.

And even more intriguing when he thought of Alicia as the mother of those children. The idea of Alicia having his baby, the image of her belly swollen with their child, filled him with a powerful and primitive longing.

He listened to her voice on the machine again and cursed her even as his heart ached.

He'd had a good life before she'd walked into his office—a job that was usually interesting, a nice apartment, a great car. Okay, maybe it wasn't a very exciting or fulfilling life, but he'd been content.

And then he'd met her, and he'd realized how much he was missing out on, how much more he wanted for his life. How much he wanted—needed—her.

Yeah, it was a scary thought—letting himself love not just Alicia but the children they might have together. But it was even scarier to imagine the rest of his life without her in it.

He jolted at the knock on the door—and was undeniably disappointed when he found his father on the other side.

He was also surprised. He could count on the fingers of one hand the number of times Lawrence Logan had stopped by his apartment, and he had to wonder at the reason for this visit now.

"Did I come at a bad time?" Lawrence asked. "Looks like you're on your way out."

Scott stared at the jacket in his hand that he hadn't even realized he'd picked up on his way to the door. He dropped it onto the arm of the sofa and glanced at the clock.

"I've got some time," he said. "Can I get you something to drink?"

His father shook his head. "No, thanks. I wasn't planning on staying long. I just stopped by to tell you that I saw an interview with that Juarez fellow on TV. The one who was just released from prison."

Scott nodded. The media had been crawling all over the story since Jack Richards was arrested, the owners of the racing team implicated, and Joe Juarez vindicated.

"Anyway, what I wanted to say to you," his father continued, "is that I'm proud of you."

Scott couldn't ever remember hearing those words from his father before, and he hadn't expected that they would mean so much to him now. He swallowed.

"I made a lot of mistakes," Lawrence continued. "Trying to steer you in directions you didn't want to go with your life. You wanted to be a cop. I couldn't understand that. When you left the police force, I thought it proved that I was right. But still, you insisted on going your own way, doing your own thing.

"You've always known what you wanted, and always had the courage to go after it. And I've finally realized that even if I don't always agree with your choices, I can respect your determination to follow your own path."

Even as his father's words soothed some of the hurt he'd lived with for so long, he wondered if they were true. Yes, there had been a time when he'd gone after what he wanted, no holds barred. But lately, it seemed all he'd been doing was running scared.

He'd come face-to-face with his greatest fear: the possibility of losing the woman he loved. But rather than face that fear, he'd pushed her away. And he realized if he really wanted to be the man his father was proud of— the man he wanted to be—he had to stop running away.

"Well, that's all I wanted to say," Lawrence told him.

"Thanks, Dad."

Because his father had taken the first step, he took the next one—he hugged him.

Chapter Fourteen

As Larry walked through the front door into his home after his brief visit with Scott, he felt a sense of inner peace and contentment that had been absent for too long. His relationship with his youngest son had always been somewhat strained. Probably his own fault, he'd finally acknowledged, because he'd never really tried to understand him.

LJ and Ryan and Jake had always been easier for him, their goals and ambitions clear. So he'd focused his attention in their direction, leaving his youngest son mostly in the care of his mother, who had no such similar difficulties.

But he felt as if he and Scott had made strides in their relationship today, and he was glad about that.

Now if only he could find a way to bridge the distance that existed with his brother.

"I thought I heard the door," Abby said, coming into the hall to greet him with a smile. "Good timing—Stella said dinner would be about half an hour, so we have time for a drink before then."

He kissed her lightly and mentally counted her as another one of the many blessings in his life. He was a fortunate man and he had a good life, and he knew he should be content with that instead of continuing to think about the brother he'd lost thirty years earlier.

His wife's gaze moved beyond him, her attention caught by something outside. "Are we expecting company?"

"Not that I know of," he said, turning to look through the window.

He squinted at the unfamiliar car—and then at the heartbreakingly familiar figure that stepped out of it.

"Ohmygod."

He hadn't realized he'd spoken aloud until he felt Abby's hand on his shoulder. "Are you all right, Larry?"

"Oh, yes, fine."

"Who—" She gasped as the man drew nearer. "Your brother?"

He wasn't surprised she'd guessed the other man's identity, even though they'd never had occasion to meet. He'd lived a lot of his early years being mistaken for the brother to whom he looked so similar.

"Yes," he admitted, just as the doorbell rang.

"Do you want me to stay or go?" she asked.

"Stay." He grasped her fingers with one hand and the doorknob with the other.

His heart was pounding wildly in his chest. Anticipation? Apprehension? He wasn't sure what he was feeling inside—there had been so many emotions over so many years, and they were now all jumbled together and crammed into this one moment.

"Hello, Larry," Terrence said.

He nodded. "Terry."

Terrence glanced at the woman at his side questioningly.

"This is my wife, Abigail," he said.

"It's a pleasure to meet you." Terrence offered his hand, which she took.

"Would you like to come in?" she asked.

Terrence glanced at him, as if expecting him to override the invitation. When he did not, his brother nodded. "Yes, I would. Thank you."

Abby nudged him away from the door so that Terrence could enter. "We were just going to have a drink in the library," she said. "Can I get you something?"

"No, that's okay. I, um, just wanted to talk to Larry for a minute."

"Of course," she said, then squeezed his hand reassuringly. "I'll just go check on dinner."

Larry watched her walk out the door and tried not to feel abandoned by her departure.

"She seems like a nice woman," Terrence said.

"I was lost for a long time after Lisanne died," he admitted. "Abby brought joy back into my life—her and the girls." He'd adopted his wife's two children after the wedding, and he'd quickly grown to love his new daughters as much as he loved his own sons.

"Children are the greatest blessing of a happy union between a man and a woman."

It wasn't just the sentiment that caused Larry to

frown, but the words that were an exact quote from his first book.

"You didn't think I'd read it, did you?"

"No, I didn't," he admitted.

"The first time, it was simply out of curiosity," he confessed. "To see what all the hype was about, and probably to scoff at the sentiments. The second time I read it was when we lost Robbie, and it scared me to realize how many truths were embodied in the pages, how many truths I'd ignored."

Larry didn't know how to respond, so he said nothing.

"Robbie's gone again," Terrence told him.

"I heard about that," he admitted gruffly. "I'm sorry for you."

"I can't help thinking that it's somehow my fault— that if I'd appreciated my family more, taken more time for them and spent fewer hours at the office, this wouldn't be happening."

He would have had to be made of stone not to respond to the anguish in his brother's voice. "I might not agree with some of the choices you made," he said, "but none of this is your fault."

"I saw something about your son, Scott, on the news," Terrence said. "He's a private investigator now?"

Larry nodded.

"I thought I might go see him, see if he can track down Robbie. Nancy, his wife, got a letter from him."

"From Las Vegas." At Terrence's startled look, he explained, "Nancy told Jake, Jake told Scott. He's already working on it."

"Oh. Nancy hired him?"

Larry shook his head. "My boys had some notion that

if they could find Robbie and bring him home, it might somehow get us talking again."

"They obviously know the importance of family."

"I like to think so."

Silence fell again, until Larry asked, "Why are you here, Terrence?"

"Because I've finally started to understand the importance of family. And we're family."

"It took you thirty years to remember that?"

His brother shrugged. "I'm a slow learner."

There was no defensiveness, no argument, and it diffused some of his own lingering resentment. "Well, better late than never, I guess."

Terrence managed a smile. Then, inexplicably, his eyes filled with tears.

"Ter?" He was as surprised as his brother when he used the nickname he hadn't spoken in more than thirty years.

His brother turned away, shook his head. "I'm sorry. It's been a hectic few months, with all the problems at the Children's Connection and Robbie's disappearance."

"There's no need to apologize," Larry said.

"I guess I finally realized that even though I couldn't make Robbie come home and put my family back together, I could make the effort to bring us back together."

"It's going to take more than an impromptu visit to erase the anger and mistrust of thirty years."

"I know," Terrence said. "But I was hoping this could be a start."

"I think it's a good start."

Terrence nodded. "Then I'll go now—before I find a way to screw it up."

This time, Larry smiled.

He walked his brother to the door. "Next time, bring your wife," he suggested. "I know Abby would like to meet her."

"I think I will." He hesitated, then offered his hand.

Larry stared at it for a moment, then took the hand and pulled his brother into a hug.

It was an awkward embrace but a heartfelt one, and both of the brother's eyes were moist when they pulled away.

As Larry closed the door behind his brother, he thought, with no small amount of satisfaction, that he'd been right. There was nothing more important than family—and he was overjoyed that he was starting to get his back.

Alicia told herself it didn't matter that Scott wasn't there for Joe's welcome home party Saturday night. He'd done the job she'd asked him to do, and her brother was home with his family. That was the only thing that mattered.

Okay, so maybe there was a gaping hole in her chest where her heart used to be, but she was sure that would heal over sometime in the next hundred years or so. In the meantime, this was a celebration.

Mrs. H. and Randy were here, and Sarajane and Jordan, and even Aster—whom she'd invited because she'd started to think of her as a friend and knew the woman would liven up any party. They were all outside in the backyard, enjoying the fresh air and mild weather and, Alicia was pleased to see, having a good time.

It was only Scott who hadn't responded to her invitation. In fact, despite her efforts to reach him at his office, his home and on his cell, she hadn't even managed to speak with him personally. She'd only left a message on his machine—putting the ball in his court, so to speak. And there it sat.

She cast a quick glance at the clock. It was already five after seven, and she'd promised the guests that dinner would be served at seven o'clock. She wasn't going to wait another minute for someone who probably wasn't going to show up anyway.

"Mmm, smells great," Joe said, bringing in the empty snack bowls.

"Chicken quesadillas with black bean salsa and Mom's Mexican lasagna."

"My favorites."

"And apple-cinnamon enchiladas for dessert."

He put his arms around her, kissed the top of her head. "What did I ever do to deserve a sister like you?"

"I guess you're just lucky," she responded lightly.

"The luckiest guy in the world," he agreed.

She managed a smile. "Why don't you call the kids in to wash up? Dinner's just about ready to go on the table."

"But Logan's not here yet."

"It doesn't matter," she said, her voice deliberately casual. "It's not his party."

"There wouldn't be a party if it wasn't for him." He tightened his arms around her. "And when I think about what could have happened at the racetrack with Richards—"

"Don't think about it," she said.

"You expect me to believe that you don't think about it?" he challenged.

"It's over and you're home," she said simply. "That's what I think about."

"I suppose you don't think about Logan, either."

She pulled out of his arms. "I love you, Joe. But you need to butt out of my life."

He tucked a stray hair behind her ear. "I admit that I had my doubts at first," he told her. "But he's a good man, Ali. Maybe even good enough for my little sister."

She sighed. "I'm not talking to you about this because there's nothing to talk about. Now go call everyone in for dinner."

But before he could do so, Lia came racing into the house, the screen door slamming shut behind her. "Scott's here and he's got a really ugly car."

And Alicia's heart—the same one that had been ripped out three days earlier—seemed to settle back inside her chest just in time to trip and fall again.

Joe grinned. "Come on, Lia," he said to his daughter. "I think we've got a few minutes before dinner will be on the table."

Alicia concentrated on her breathing as she took the quesadillas out of the oven. She wasn't going to let his presence affect her, wasn't going to overreact to his decision to come.

She heard him speak to her brother and niece on the back porch, the usual exchange of pleasantries. Then the door opened again, and closed quietly, and she knew it wasn't Joey or Lia who had come inside. Of course, the sudden nerves dancing over her skin were a bigger clue than the absence of a slamming door, but she was determined to ignore those.

"Hi, Alicia."

Her traitorous heart was pounding so loudly it was a wonder he couldn't hear it from clear across the room, but she managed to turn around slowly, speak casually. "I didn't think you were coming."

"Neither did I," he admitted.

"Why did you?"

He paused for a minute, then said, "I bought a '68 Z28 Camaro."

"You came here to tell me that?"

"I brought it here to show you."

"Lia said it's ugly." It hurt to look at him and still want him so much, to wish so desperately that things might have turned out differently. So she turned away and busied herself cutting the quesadillas into wedges, then arranging them on a plate.

"It needs a lot of work," he admitted. "Probably more than the Corvette ever did."

"That will keep you busy," she said, even as she wondered how long she could keep up this inane conversation without falling apart.

"When I bought the Stingray, I could picture exactly how I wanted it to look when I was done," he told her. "But the whole time I was working on it, I doubted that I had either the patience or perseverance to do it right.

"I don't think anyone was more surprised than I was when it was done. Apparently I have a lot of fortitude when it comes to the things that matter to me."

She wasn't sure where he was going with his rambling and didn't dare let herself hope. Her emotions had been trampled too many times for her to take a chance again.

"If you want to talk cars, you'd be better off talking to my brother. He could—"

"I'm not talking about cars," he interrupted.

She raised her eyebrows as she carried the plate to the table.

"Okay, I am. But it's not just about cars. It's about us."

"Us?" Her heart did a funny little skip and jump.

"In a lot of ways, our relationship is like the Camaro outside."

"Huh?" She got the salsa from the fridge and put it on the table with the quesadillas.

"I'm really messing this up, aren't I?"

"I don't know," she admitted. "I'm having a little trouble following your thoughts."

"Could you stop fussing and look at me for a minute?"

"I'm behind schedule with dinner. I really need…" Her words trailed off when his hands came down on her shoulders.

Gently but firmly, he turned her around to face him. And oh, it felt so good to have him touching her again— even if the touch was casual and impersonal.

"A classic vehicle like that is a commitment," he said. "You can't buy it and then walk away. Just like you can't tell someone you love them and then walk away."

"I can't believe you're comparing love to a Camaro."

"They're both commitments."

"And buying this car has suddenly made you an expert on commitment?" she challenged.

His hands dropped away and he stuffed them into his pockets. "I came here to tell you something," he said. "But once I say it, it's done. It can't be taken back or ignored. We'll both have to deal with it."

"Then say it."

But he remained silent for a moment, then when he

did speak, his voice was tinged with both annoyance and accusation. "You let me walk away."

She met his gaze evenly. "That was your choice."

He stared at her hard, his eyes narrowed. "But you said you loved me."

"I do love you," she said. "Too much to try to make you stay somewhere you didn't want to be."

"What if I've decided that I want to be with you?" he finally asked.

She swallowed. "Have you?"

His smile was wry. "I should have known you wouldn't make this easy for me."

"Do you want it to be easy?"

"I want *you,* Alicia."

Her heart skipped and jumped again.

"And if I stay," he continued, "if you decide to give me another chance, you have to understand that I'm not as open-minded as you."

"Meaning?"

He reached for her again, taking her hands this time. "I won't ever let you walk away."

Her lips started to curve, and her heart started to heal. "Are you going to say it, or are you going to continue talking circles around it all night?"

"I'm warming up to it."

She waited.

"I didn't think I could love anyone." He brought her hands to his lips and kissed them, first one, then the other. "I didn't want to love anyone.

"Now, I can't imagine not loving you." He dipped his head and touched his lips to hers, softly, gently. "I do love you, Alicia."

Her smile widened. "Was that so difficult to admit?"

"Not when I considered that the alternative was living my life without you." He kissed her again, longer, deeper, lingering. "How is it that you seemed to figure out my feelings before I did?"

"It was your car," she told him.

He pulled back slightly to look at her.

"The Corvette," she explained. "I expected you would have been furious, or at least upset, that it had blown up. But when I asked you about it, you said it was just a set of wheels.

"I knew how much that car meant to you, how restoring it became your focus after Freddie was killed. And then you just shrugged it off—not because it didn't matter, I realized, but because I mattered more."

"You think you're pretty smart, don't you?"

"Am I wrong?"

"No, you're exactly right. When I saw you on the ground, unconscious and bleeding—" He shook his head. "Even now, I can't remember that moment without icy fear gripping my heart.

"Yeah, you matter more than anything else. More than I ever could have imagined."

"Does that mean you want to hang around and see where this goes?" she asked.

He finally released her hands to wrap his arms around her. "I already know where I want it to go."

"Yeah?"

"And I want it tangled up with all kinds of messy emotions."

"Already there," she told him.

"You still love me—even though I was an idiot?"

"I can't turn off my emotions like a tap," she reminded him. "So, yes, I still love you."

He tightened his arms around her. "I can't promise you forever, but I can promise that I'll love you for as long as my heart is beating inside of me, because that heart belongs to you."

"That's good enough for me."

"Then you'll marry me?" he asked.

And she'd thought he couldn't say or do anything else that would surprise her today—but this certainly did.

She swallowed. "Is that a proposal?"

He smiled. "Yeah."

"Then…yeah." She pressed her lips to his.

"Since this is a day of revelations, there's something else I should tell you."

"What's that?"

"I want kids."

And her heart—now completely healed and feeling so full inside her chest she thought it might burst— simply overflowed.

"You want kids?"

He nodded. "As many as you think we can handle—but we can wait until you graduate to get started, if you want."

"You want me to finish school?"

"I love who you are right now," he said. "But I know being a doctor has been a dream of yours for a long time, and I want you to do whatever makes you happy."

"Dr. Juarez," she whispered the name, as she'd been doing for so many years. Then she shook her head. "I don't know. It's still a long journey and—"

"No road is too long if it takes you where you want to go," he assured her.

"You're going to be on that road with me?"

"Every step of the way," he promised. "But I'd like you to consider Dr. Logan instead of Dr. Juarez."

"Aren't there enough doctors in your family already?" she teased.

"Maybe, but I want one that's just mine."

"Then we'll have to see what we can do about that."

He kissed her again, and it was a promise as much as a kiss, a pledge that joined them together. And she kissed him back, with all of the love and hope and healing that were in her heart.

When they finally drew apart, both a little breathless, the sun was starting to set. But it wasn't the end of a day for them—it was the beginning of a life together.

* * * * *

Don't miss the final installment of the new
Special Edition continuity
LOGAN'S LEGACY REVISITED.
Jillian Logan knew Mr. Right was worth waiting for.
But can their relationship survive after she discovers
that journalist Gil Reynolds had something to do with
the media attacks on her family?
Look for ALWAYS A BRIDESMAID
by reader favorite Kristin Hardy
On sale June 2007
wherever Silhouette Books are sold.

Mediterranean Nights

Join the guests and crew of **Alexandra's Dream,**
*the newest luxury ship to set sail on the romantic
Mediterranean, as they experience the glamorous
world of cruising.*

*A new Harlequin continuity series
begins in June 2007 with
FROM RUSSIA, WITH LOVE
by Ingrid Weaver*

*Marina Artamova books a cabin on the luxurious
cruise ship* **Alexandra's Dream,** *when she finds out
that her orphaned nephew and his adoptive father
are aboard. She's determined to be reunited with
the boy…but the romantic ambience of the ship and
her undeniable attraction to a man she considers
her enemy are about to interfere with her quest!*

Turn the page for a sneak preview!

Piraeus, Greece

"THERE SHE IS, Stefan. *Alexandra's Dream*." David Anderson squatted beside his new son and pointed at the dark blue hull that towered above the pier. The cruise ship was a majestic sight, twelve decks high and as long as a city block. A circle of silver and gold stars, the logo of the Liberty Cruise Line, gleamed from the swept-back smokestack. Like some legendary sea creature born for the water, the ship emanated power from every sleek curve—even at rest it held the promise of motion. "That's going to be our home for the next ten days."

The child beside him remained silent, his cheeks working in and out as he sucked furiously on his thumb. Hair so blond it appeared white ruffled against his forehead in the harbor breeze. The baby-sweet scent unique to the very young mingled with the tang of the sea.

"Ship," David said. "Uh, *parakhod.*"

From beneath his bangs, Stefan looked at the *Alexandra's Dream.* Although he didn't release his thumb, the corners of his mouth tightened with the beginning of a smile.

David grinned. That was Stefan's first smile this afternoon, one of only two since they had left the orphanage yesterday. It was probably because of the boat—according to the orphanage staff, the boy loved boats, which was the main reason David had decided to book this cruise. Then again, there was a strong possibility the smile could have been a reaction to David's attempt at pocket-dictionary Russian. Whatever the cause, it was a good start.

The liaison from the adoption agency had claimed that Stefan had been taught some English, but David had yet to see evidence of it. David continued to speak, positive his son would understand his tone even if he couldn't grasp the words. "This is her maiden voyage. Her first trip, just like this is our first trip, and that makes it special." He motioned toward the stage that had been set up on the pier beneath the ship's bow. "That's why everyone's celebrating."

The ship's official christening ceremony had been held the day before and had been a closed affair, with only the cruise-line executives and VIP guests invited, but the stage hadn't yet been disassembled. Banners bearing the blue and white of the Greek flag of the ship's owner, as well as the Liberty circle of stars logo, draped the edges of the platform. In the center, a group of musicians and a dance troupe dressed in traditional white folk costumes performed for the benefit of the *Alexandra's Dream*'s first passengers. Their audience was in a festive mood, snapping their fingers in time to the music while the dancers twirled and wove through their steps.

David bobbed his head to the rhythm of the mandolins. They were playing a folk tune that seemed vaguely familiar, possibly from a movie he'd seen. He hummed a few notes. "Catchy melody, isn't it?"

Stefan turned his gaze on David. His eyes were a striking shade of blue, as cool and pale as a winter horizon and far too solemn for a child not yet five. Still, the smile that hovered at the corners of his mouth persisted. He moved his head with the music, mirroring David's motion.

David gave a silent cheer at the interaction. Hopefully, this cruise would provide countless opportunities for more. "Hey, good for you," he said. "Do you like the music?"

The child's eyes sparked. He withdrew his thumb with a pop. *"Moozika!"*

"Music. Right!" David held out his hand. "Come on, let's go closer so we can watch the dancers."

Stefan grasped David's hand quickly, as if he feared it would be withdrawn. In an instant his budding smile was replaced by a look close to panic.

Did he remember the car accident that had killed his parents? It would be a mercy if he didn't. As far as David knew, Stefan had never spoken of it to anyone. Whatever he had seen had made him run so far from the crash that the police hadn't found him until the next day. The event had traumatized him to the extent that he hadn't uttered a word until his fifth week at the orphanage. Even now he seldom talked.

David sat back on his heels and brushed the hair from Stefan's forehead. That solemn, too-old gaze locked with his, and for an instant, David felt as if he looked back in time at an image of himself thirty years ago.

He didn't need to speak the same language to understand exactly how this boy felt. He knew what it meant to be alone and powerless among strangers, trying to be brave and tough but wishing with every fiber of his being for a place to belong, to be safe, and most of all for someone to love him….

He knew in his heart he would be a good parent to Stefan. It was why he had never considered halting the adoption process after Ellie had left him. He hadn't balked when he'd learned of the recent claim by Stefan's spinster aunt, either; the absentee relative had shown up too late for her case to be considered. The adoption was meant to be. He and this child already shared a bond that went deeper than paperwork or legalities.

A seagull screeched overhead, making Stefan start and press closer to David.

"That's my boy," David murmured. He swallowed hard, struck by the simple truth of what he had just said.

That's my boy.

"I CAN'T BE PATIENT, RUDOLPH. I'm not going to stand by and watch my nephew get ripped from his country and his roots to live on the other side of the world."

Rudolph hissed out a slow breath. "Marina, I don't like the sound of that. What are you planning?"

"I'm going to talk some sense into this American kidnapper."

"No. Absolutely not. No offence, but diplomacy is not your strong suit."

"Diplomacy be damned. Their ship's due to sail at five o'clock."

"Then you wouldn't have an opportunity to speak with him even if his lawyer agreed to a meeting."

"I'll have ten days of opportunities, Rudolph, since I plan to be on board that ship."

* * * * *

*Follow Marina and David as they join forces
to uncover the reason behind little Stefan's unusual
silence, and the secret behind the death
of his parents....*

*Look for FROM RUSSIA, WITH LOVE
by Ingrid Weaver
in stores June 2007.*

HARLEQUIN®

Mediterranean NIGHTS™

Tycoon Elias Stamos is launching his newest luxury cruise ship from his home port in Greece. But someone from his past is eager to expose old secrets and to see the Stamos empire crumble.

Mediterranean Nights
launches in June 2007 with...

FROM RUSSIA, WITH LOVE
by *Ingrid Weaver*

Join the guests and crew of *Alexandra's Dream* as they are drawn into a world of glamour, romance and intrigue in this new 12-book series.

HARLEQUIN®

///// NASCAR®

In February...

**Collect all 4 debut novels in
the Harlequin NASCAR series.**

SPEED DATING
by *USA TODAY* bestselling author
Nancy Warren

On sale February 2007

THUNDERSTRUCK
by Roxanne St. Claire

HEARTS UNDER CAUTION
by Gina Wilkins

DANGER ZONE
by Debra Webb

And in May don't miss...

Gabby, a gutsy female NASCAR driver,
can't believe her mother is harping at her
again. How many times does she have
to say it? She's not going to help run the
family's corporation. She's not shopping
for a husband of the right pedigree. And
there's no way she's giving up racing!

SPEED BUMPS *is one of four
exciting Harlequin NASCAR books that
will go on sale in May.*

SEE COUPON INSIDE.

www.GetYourHeartRacing.com   NASCARMAY

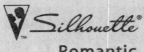

REQUEST YOUR FREE BOOKS!
2 FREE NOVELS PLUS 2 FREE GIFTS!

SPECIAL EDITION®

Life, Love and Family!

YES! Please send me 2 FREE Silhouette Special Edition® novels and my 2 FREE gifts. After receiving them, if I don't wish to receive any more books, I can return the shipping statement marked "cancel." If I don't cancel, I will receive 6 brand-new novels every month and be billed just $4.24 per book in the U.S., or $4.99 per book in Canada, plus 25¢ shipping and handling per book and applicable taxes, if any*. That's a savings of at least 15% off the cover price! I understand that accepting the 2 free books and gifts places me under no obligation to buy anything. I can always return a shipment and cancel at any time. Even if I never buy another book from Silhouette, the two free books and gifts are mine to keep forever.

235 SDN EEYU   335 SDN EEY6

Name _____ (PLEASE PRINT)

Address _____ Apt. _____

City _____ State/Prov. _____ Zip/Postal Code _____

Signature (if under 18, a parent or guardian must sign)

Mail to the Silhouette Reader Service™:
IN U.S.A.: P.O. Box 1867, Buffalo, NY 14240-1867
IN CANADA: P.O. Box 609, Fort Erie, Ontario L2A 5X3

Not valid to current Silhouette Special Edition subscribers.

Want to try two free books from another line?
Call 1-800-873-8635 or visit www.morefreebooks.com.

* Terms and prices subject to change without notice. NY residents add applicable sales tax. Canadian residents will be charged applicable provincial taxes and GST. This offer is limited to one order per household. All orders subject to approval. Credit or debit balances in a customer's account(s) may be offset by any other outstanding balance owed by or to the customer. Please allow 4 to 6 weeks for delivery.

Your Privacy: Silhouette is committed to protecting your privacy. Our Privacy Policy is available online at www.eHarlequin.com or upon request from the Reader Service. From time to time we make our lists of customers available to reputable firms who may have a product or service of interest to you. If you would prefer we not share your name and address, please check here. ☐

SSE07

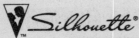

COMING NEXT MONTH

SSECNM0507